Serendipity of Fiction Concepts

Micro Stories of Hope, Winter Magic and Quiet Transformations

Morgan Hale

Contents

Introduction: On the Brightness of Small Stories

Stories shape the way we understand
the world.

They are the maps we consult when the path ahead is unclear, the lanterns we hold when the dark grows close. Some stories stride toward us with great ambition, dressed in sweeping plots and long journeys. Others arrive with far less ceremony.

They step quietly into view, offering only a brief moment, a single gesture or an unexpected image, then leave us changed in a way we often notice only later. This collection belongs to that smaller and more deliberate tradition, a tradition that knows a whisper can carry as much weight as a shout.

Introduction: On the Brightness of Small Stories

Micro stories ask for a particular kind of presence.
They move swiftly but open slowly.

> In limited space they attempt
> something generous: to condense a
> world into a fragment and trust the
> reader to complete the rest.

A micro story may be only a page long, yet it can hold
the pulse of a whole life. It may appear simple, but
simplicity is not the absence of depth. It is the
invitation to look closer. These pieces rely on what is
not stated, on what exists in the white space
surrounding each word, on the shadow that hints at
something just beyond reach. They meet the reader in
that borderland between suggestion and
understanding, where imagination does its quiet
work.

We live in a world that moves quickly. Attention
scatters, days blur, and the constant hum of
information fills the air. In such times, the short form
offers a welcome pause.

> It does not demand hours. It asks only
> for a moment of focus, a steady
> breath, a willingness to listen.

Within that pause, something soft but insistent can
unfold. A single image, a small revelation or a fleeting
emotion can catch the reader by surprise. This

subtlety is the strength of micro fiction. It values concentration over scale and resonance over volume. Its brevity is not a limitation. It is an art of precision.

The eighty stories in this book were shaped with that belief in mind. They were written to be read in a single sitting or many small ones, to be visited and revisited, to linger quietly like traces of light on a winter morning.

> They explore hope, winter magic, serendipity and quiet transformations, four themes that emerge naturally from the kind of attention micro fiction encourages.

These themes are not separate rooms so much as connected corridors. Each story stands alone, but together they form a passage through tender spaces of the human experience.

The journey begins with **hope**, a subject both delicate and resilient. Hope rarely announces itself with fanfare. More often it hides in corners, waiting patiently to be noticed. It appears in the courage of ordinary people who rise each day to face whatever comes.

> It shows itself in the unspoken kindness between strangers or the unexpected warmth that blooms in times of uncertainty.

Introduction: On the Brightness of Small Stories

In these opening stories, hope is not a distant promise but something already woven into the landscape of daily life. It can look like endurance. It can look like forgiveness. It can look like the smallest step toward a better moment. If hope were a color, it would be the faint glow that precedes dawn, subtle enough to miss, yet unmistakable once seen.

From hope the collection moves into **winter magic**, where the season itself becomes a storyteller. Winter narrows the world to essentials. Trees stand bare, breath hangs in the air, light fades early and returns reluctantly. Yet in this stripped down setting, attention sharpens.

> Winter is a season that leaves room for wonder.

It invites us to notice the textures of frost, the quiet under snowfall, the glimmer that comes from stillness. Its enchantments are gentle rather than dramatic. In these stories, winter becomes a place where the boundaries thin and possibilities slip through. A conversation may carry more weight than expected. A familiar street may feel changed by nightfall. The world may reveal a secret it has kept for years. Winter has always held a quiet magic, and here it unfolds in small yet vivid moments.

After winter magic comes **serendipity**, the art of fortunate missteps. Serendipity thrives on surprises, the accidental alignments that shape our days without warning. It is the missed bus that leads to a meaningful meeting, the odd object found at the bottom of a drawer, the long forgotten message that arrives exactly when needed. Serendipity is neither grand destiny nor chaos.

It is the delicate pattern that emerges
when unrelated moments lean
gently toward one another.

These stories explore how lives intersect in improbable ways, how coincidence can feel like guidance and how a single unexpected turn can tilt an entire day, or an entire life, toward something better.

The final section, **quiet transformations**, turns inward. Change is often portrayed as sudden and dramatic, but most real transformations are soft. They unfold slowly, almost imperceptibly. People shift their understanding of themselves, revise their memories, soften their grief or allow something long held to finally rest.

In these stories, change does not arrive
with thunder.

It appears in the silence after an argument, in the moment someone sees their reflection with new eyes or in the gentle fading of an old fear. Quiet transformation is the steady hand of hindsight, the tender work of rebuilding or the relief of letting go. It is the recognition that life rarely turns on a hinge but rather on a collection of small, steady pivots.

These four threads weave through the book in their own rhythm, but they also echo one another. Hope often leads to transformation. Winter magic often feels like serendipity. Serendipity can spark hope. Transformation can feel like an enchantment. They are distinct ideas, yet deeply connected, much like the brief stories that explore them. The collection moves through these moods the way a season moves toward another, slowly and naturally.

Reading micro fiction is a little like stepping into a room filled with windows.

> Each piece reflects a different angle of
> the world, and every reader will see
> something unique through the glass.

A story of hope may remind one reader of a moment from childhood. A winter tale may evoke the quiet of a long ago evening. A serendipitous encounter may echo a coincidence from years past. A quiet transformation may reveal a truth a reader did not know they were looking for. Short stories, especially very short ones, leave room for the reader to bring their own life into the conversation.

There is also a particular pleasure in returning to micro fiction. Because the pieces are small, they can be revisited easily. A story read in the morning may feel different at night. A story read in winter may glow differently in spring. Their shapes shift with context, like small objects held to the light. What they reveal depends on where the reader stands.

This book was written with February in mind, a month that carries its own kind of tension. Winter is still strong, yet the first hints of change begin to stir. The days lengthen quietly. The light alters just enough to notice. February is a month of thresholds. It invites reflection but also whispers of renewal. It asks us to consider what we have endured and what we are becoming. It is the perfect time for small stories that illuminate the spaces between stillness and movement.

Stories, no matter how brief, are companions.

They walk beside us for a while, offering company, comfort or challenge.

They can shift our mood, steady our thoughts or inspire us to look again at something we thought we understood. My hope is that the stories in this collection offer such companionship. That they bring warmth to cold days and clarity to uncertain ones. That they encourage a closer look at the quiet miracles scattered throughout ordinary life.

When you finish a micro story, you often carry a trace of it into your day. Sometimes it is a feeling.

Sometimes it is a question. Sometimes it is simply the lingering sense that the world has more depth than it revealed at first glance. These traces matter. They shape the way we move through the world, how we listen, how we hope. They grow in the margins where thought meets imagination.

> May these stories offer traces that stay
> with you.

May they brighten your moments in small but meaningful ways. And may they remind you that even the briefest story can carry a spark strong enough to warm the heart, illuminate a path or open a door that had gone unnoticed.

Welcome.

The journey begins.

Chapter 1
HOPE

Some lights are small,
but steady in the dark.
They do not promise miracles,
only one more gentle step.

Lantern on the Third Floor

Every evening at seven, the woman in the third floor window lit a small lantern and set it on the sill. No one in the building knew why. Some said it was decorative. Others guessed it was for a cat that had passed away, a ritual of remembrance. A few joked that she was guiding lost ships home, though the nearest ocean was miles away. No one asked her directly. People in the building nodded politely but kept mostly to themselves.

Jonas, who lived across the courtyard, often noticed the lantern while making dinner. He had been laid off months earlier and had not yet told his family. Each night after sunset, he sat at the table with bills and rejection emails piled around him. The lantern's small glow became a strange comfort, a reminder that someone else was awake, someone else was quietly enduring something too.

One night, when everything felt especially heavy, the lantern did not appear. Seven came and went. Eight. Nine. All darkness. Jonas found himself standing at his window, palms pressed lightly against the cold glass. He tried to reason with himself. People forget things. People go out. People change routines. Still, the missing glow unsettled him more than he expected.

By ten, he made tea for no reason other than to keep himself busy. He walked back to the window with the mug cupped in both hands and there it was. A soft flame blooming in the dark, as if it had been waiting for him to return. The relief surprised him. It spread like warmth through his chest, a slow exhale he did not know he had been holding.

The next day, on his way out, he found a small paper taped to the lobby doors. It read:

"Thank you to whoever watches my lantern. I had the flu this week but I'm feeling better. Your attention kept me company."

No name. No apartment number. Just a thin sheet of paper with handwriting that tilted upward, as if reaching for something brighter.

Jonas folded the note and placed it in his coat pocket. Later, while updating his resume for the hundredth time, he felt the paper against his fingers and smiled. A quiet truth settled into him. Even without knowing it, people can carry each other. Even in a world of closed doors and private burdens, a small light can travel farther than expected.

And that was enough to begin again the next morning.

The Color of Quiet Mornings

Mara began painting again in late February, though she hadn't touched a brush in years. The paints had been packed away in a shoebox under her bed, old and cracked around the edges, the lids stiff with dust. She had stopped once life grew too busy and too loud. There had always been something else demanding attention, something louder than the quiet urge to create.

But one morning she woke early. The light in the kitchen was a soft blue, the kind that makes everything appear gentler than it is. She sat with her tea and felt a small gap inside, a pause she had not known she needed. On a whim, she pulled the box from beneath her bed, carried it to the table and opened it like a door she had once locked.

The first strokes were hesitant. The paint dragged unevenly. The brush felt unfamiliar. She tried to paint a bowl of fruit but it turned into something else entirely, something abstract and shy. She nearly threw it away until she noticed a streak of gold she had not consciously added. It shimmered faintly in the morning light, a soft reminder that not everything needed to be deliberate to be beautiful.

Over the next weeks she rose earlier and earlier, not out of discipline but out of desire. These quiet mornings became a kind of refuge. The world felt lighter before sunrise, and her thoughts did too. She painted colors she didn't have names for, shapes that curved and tangled, emotions she had never tried to capture before. Each canvas became a small conversation with herself.

One morning, while tidying the table, she realised she had filled an entire stack with finished pieces. Not perfect, not polished, but real. Honest. Hers.

She carried them to the window and set them in the sun. Outside, a neighbor walking his dog paused and looked up. "These are yours?" he called.

Mara nodded, embarrassed.

"They're beautiful," he said. "Bright. I can see them from the street some days. They make the block feel softer."

She hadn't expected that. She hadn't expected anyone to notice. But someone had. Someone saw her small attempt to reclaim something lost.

After he walked away, she looked again at the paintings. They seemed new. Not larger, not more impressive, but alive. Proof that even after a long silence, creation can return. That something neglected can bloom again with the slightest bit of attention.

And in that moment, Mara understood that hope has a color. It looks a little like morning light reflected on unfinished canvases.

The Bridge at Early Dawn

Sam crossed the old footbridge every morning before work. It was the long route, not the logical one, but he preferred it. The wooden boards creaked in a way that reminded him of childhood summers spent near lakes. The river beneath moved slowly, heavy with winter melt. The bridge had become a place to gather his thoughts before the day began.

He had been carrying a private heaviness for months. A friendship that ended abruptly. A dream he had let go of without meaning to. The kind of quiet grief that doesn't demand attention but never truly leaves.

One morning, as he stepped onto the bridge, he noticed a small wooden box resting on the railing. It was simple, unmarked, barely larger than his palm.

He glanced around. No one in sight. Curiosity nudged him forward. He lifted the lid.

Inside lay a folded note and a single dried flower. The note read:

"For whoever needs this today. You are not walking alone."

Sam looked at the handwriting. Neat, rounded, anonymous. The flower was pale yellow, delicate but intact, as if it had been kept safe for years.

He closed the box and held it for a moment, feeling an unexpected warmth settle into him. He didn't know who had left it, or how many people had passed without noticing. But it was here now, and he had found it, or it had found him.

He placed the box back exactly as he had discovered it and continued across the bridge. The boards creaked under his feet, familiar and steady. Something inside him felt slightly loosened, as if a knot had eased.

Over the following weeks he kept crossing the bridge, half expecting the box to vanish. But it remained, sometimes with different notes tucked inside. Small messages. Gentle reminders. Words left by someone who understood the quiet weight people carry.

One morning, without fully deciding to, Sam added his own note. He wrote only a few words, something simple but sincere:

"It gets lighter. Even if slowly."

He slipped it into the box and walked on. The sun was rising, the sky brightening in soft colors. The river moved steadily beneath him.

For the first time in a long while, dawn felt like a beginning rather than a repetition. And that was hope enough.

The Window with the Paper Birds

Every spring, months before real birds returned to the neighborhood, Mrs. Alden filled her front window with paper ones. She folded them from old newspapers, maps, sheet music and the pastel wrappers from the bakery down the street. Some were perched, some mid flight, some balancing on invisible currents of air. The window looked like a captured breeze.

People passing by always slowed their steps. Children pointed. Adults smiled without meaning to. No one quite knew why she made them. Some guessed she was lonely. Others imagined she had once been an art teacher. The truth was simpler. She liked the idea that hope could have wings made of anything at all.

Nina, who lived across the street, watched the display change each week. She had been struggling through a difficult season, the kind that arrived quietly and accumulated until even getting dressed felt heavy. She often stood at her own window late at night, drawn to the silhouettes of the paper birds glowing faintly under the streetlamp.

One afternoon she gathered the courage to cross the street and knock. Mrs. Alden opened the door with a smile that felt like sunlight. When Nina complimented the birds, the older woman stepped aside and said, "Come look closely. They're better up close."

Inside, Nina saw dozens more on the dining table, mid fold. Some made from recipes, others from letters, some from old lottery tickets. Each one imperfect, edges slightly crooked, but full of intention.

"They're beautiful," Nina said.

"They're reminders," Mrs. Alden replied. "Every year I choose scraps that would have been thrown away. I fold them into something that can look forward. It helps me remember that nothing is finished until we say it is."

Nina ran her fingers lightly over a bird made from a map. A single crease shimmered in the light. Something eased in her chest.

"Take one," Mrs. Alden said. "Choose whichever one you need."

Nina selected a small blue bird made from the corner of an envelope. She carried it home carefully, as if it might take flight. She set it on her windowsill where daylight could reach it.

The next morning, she woke earlier than usual. The blue bird caught the rising sun and seemed to glow. She felt something shift inside, subtle but real.

And for the first time in many months, her day began with the quiet idea that she, too, could be folded into something new.

The Last Cup in the Café

The café opened at six each morning, but Elias always arrived at five fifty. He liked the moments before the rush, the hum of refrigerators, the soft clink of the barista setting out mugs. The café was small, tucked between a laundromat and a closed down shoe repair shop. Most people walked past without noticing it, but to Elias it felt like a pocket of calm carved out of the city's noise.

He always ordered the same thing, chamomile tea with honey. The barista, Liora, never asked for his order anymore. She simply greeted him with a gentle nod and set the kettle on. Their conversations were brief but warm, small exchanges that made the morning feel steady.

One day, the café door stuck when he pulled it open. A handwritten sign hung in the window: "Closing next week. Thank you for the memories." Inside, the display shelves were half empty, and the usual sound of the radio was absent. Liora offered a tired smile.

"Lease went up again," she said. "We held on as long as we could."

Elias felt a pang he couldn't fully explain. This place had been an anchor during a year when everything else had shifted beneath him. He took his usual seat while Liora prepared his tea. The steam rose in soft curls, and the honey glowed like late afternoon light.

Across the room, a young couple read the sign with disappointment. An older man sighed, removing his glasses. A woman in a paint smeared coat stood frozen in the doorway. Everyone seemed to feel the loss of something they hadn't known they depended on.

When Liora stepped out from behind the counter, she held a small box. She placed it in front of Elias. "You're here every morning. You understand why this place mattered. I want you to have something."

Inside the box was the last ceramic mug they had ever ordered, deep green with a chipped rim.

"It's imperfect," she said. "But it's the one everyone reached for when they needed comfort."

Elias touched the warm ceramic. "Thank you," he said, though the words felt too small.

For the rest of the week, the café filled with quiet goodbyes. People shared stories. They left drawings on napkins, notes of gratitude, spare change in the tip jar even when they had no order. A strange thing happened. The place seemed to glow brighter in its final days than in all the years before.

The evening it closed, Elias walked home with the green mug wrapped carefully in his coat. It was chipped, imperfect, ordinary. Yet holding it, he felt a small ember of hope catch inside him.

Some places close. Some seasons end. But the warmth they create can be carried long after the doors lock for the last time.

A Letter for Tomorrow

Tara had a habit of writing letters she never intended to send. She kept them in a wooden box under her bed, each sealed in an envelope without a name. They were written to people she had known, people she might one day meet, and sometimes to no one in particular. She wrote when her thoughts tangled, when worry pressed too tightly, or when she felt the need to speak without interruption.

One evening, during a particularly restless winter, she wrote a letter that felt different. It was not a confession or a memory. It was a message to her future self. She wrote about the small courage it takes to continue. She wrote about the things she hoped to grow into. She wrote about the light she believed still waited somewhere ahead, even if faint.

When she finished, she sealed the envelope and wrote one word on the front: Tomorrow.

She placed it in the box with the others, thinking little of it. But the next morning, the word lingered in her thoughts. It followed her as she drank her tea, as she walked to work, as she completed tasks that felt heavier than they should. Tomorrow, the letter seemed to whisper. Keep walking toward tomorrow.

For weeks she carried that quiet message with her. On hard days, she touched the box before leaving the house. On good days, she added small notes of gratitude, folding them into the corners of her pockets. Slowly, almost invisibly, her outlook shifted. Not dramatically. Just enough to breathe easier.

One late evening, after a long day that left her drained, Tara opened the box. The envelope rested on top, waiting. She hesitated. Part of her feared the letter might no longer fit the person she was becoming. But she opened it anyway.

The handwriting looked different from how she remembered. Softer. More certain. As she read, she felt something loosen within her. The words were gentle, filled with hope she hadn't realised she possessed. Her past self had written not out of despair but out of belief, trusting that the future would hold something worth meeting.

When she reached the end, she smiled. She placed the letter back into the box, but this time she did not seal it away. She left the lid slightly open, letting the message breathe.

Tomorrow was no longer a distant horizon. It had become a companion, a direction, a promise she was willing to follow.

And with that simple realization, she felt the first true warmth of spring stirring quietly inside her.

The Library at the End of the Street

The old library at the end of the street was scheduled to close in June. The wooden doors had warped, the roof needed repair and the funding never seemed to arrive. Most people had heard the news, sighed and moved on. But for Nora, the library had been a lifeline during a difficult spring, and she visited every week with a devotion that surprised even her.

The librarian, Mr. Hale, greeted her with the same gentle nod each time. He had worked there for more than thirty years. He moved slowly now, pausing to rest between tasks, yet his eyes always brightened when someone walked in. The library might have been fading, but he carried a quiet belief that it still mattered.

One rainy afternoon Nora found him stacking books into cardboard boxes.

"Are these being sold?" she asked.

"Donated," he replied. "It hurts less to think of them finding new homes."

She helped him lift a stack of biographies. They worked together in silence until she noticed a small notebook near the checkout desk. It was filled with handwritten notes from patrons. Tiny messages. Thank you for a quiet place to breathe. Thank you for teaching me how to find my first novel. Thank you for remembering my son's name.

"People left these for you?" she asked.

"For the library," he said with a smile. "I plan to read one each night until the doors close."

Nora held the notebook for a long moment. She felt an ache behind her ribs. She did not want this place to vanish. Not the worn carpets or the soft lamps or the comforting hush that greeted her at the door.

That evening, she wrote a message of her own. She returned the next day and slipped it into the notebook when Mr. Hale was shelving returns. She did not intend to be seen, yet he noticed her gesture and nodded once. A quiet thank you that warmed her through.

Two weeks later, something unexpected happened. Someone posted a photo of the notebook online. Within days, the library received a small grant and a flood of volunteer offers. One local carpenter repaired the warped doors. A contractor patched the roof at cost. Parents formed a reading group. Students organized a fundraiser.

By June, the library remained open, not fully saved but steady enough to continue. On the first day of summer, Mr. Hale placed the notebook back on the desk without any fanfare.

Nora visited that afternoon. Children played in the aisles. Volunteers carried ladders. The lights glowed softly against the shelves.

Mr. Hale clasped his hands behind his back. "Hope is not loud," he said. "It simply waits for enough people to notice it."

Nora believed him. She always had.

The Bench Beside the Bakery

There was a bench beside the bakery that no one seemed to claim. It sat half in shade, half in sunlight, with peeling blue paint that gave it a lived in charm. People used it for quick rests, short phone calls or tying shoelaces before rushing off. No one stayed long.

Except Leo. He visited the bench every afternoon after work with a book he rarely opened. The bakery aroma drifted through the air, warm and sweet. The bench felt like a small island where the world slowed just enough for him to breathe.

One afternoon he noticed an elderly woman standing nearby, leaning slightly on her cane. She seemed out of breath, so Leo offered the seat. She accepted with a grateful smile.

They sat together in comfortable silence. After a while she said, "This bench has been here longer than the bakery. People forget, but it used to be the only place to rest on this street."

Leo smiled. "It still feels like a resting place."

The woman nodded. "A good bench listens without judgment."

Over the next weeks Leo saw her often. Her name was Helena. She liked lemon pastries, knitted scarves for rescue animals and believed every person carried at least one story worth hearing. Leo found himself looking forward to their brief conversations. Something about her presence softened the edges of his days.

One chilly afternoon, he arrived to find the bench empty but a small envelope resting on the seat. His name was written on it. Inside was a note from Helena.

"Dear Leo. Thank you for sharing this bench with me. I am moving to live with my daughter. I wanted to leave you a gift. Not money or objects. Just this thought. Every place becomes kinder when someone chooses to pause there. You made this bench kinder. Do the same wherever you go."

Her handwriting trembled slightly, but her message felt steady and bright.

Leo folded the note and sat down. The bakery door opened and closed. People hurried past. The afternoon light shifted. He felt a gentle warmth settle inside him.

From that day onward, Leo approached each moment with quiet intention. He greeted strangers more often. He helped a neighbor carry groceries. He offered his seat to tired commuters. Small gestures that cost nothing but returned something meaningful.

And each time he passed the little blue bench, he touched the backrest softly, as if thanking it for introducing him to the idea that hope can begin in a simple place where two people choose to sit together.

The Umbrella at the Bus Stop

Rain had begun as a light drizzle but quickly grew into a steady downpour. The bus stop provided only a narrow patch of shelter, barely enough for one person. Mira stood shivering, clutching her bag, resigned to the cold.

A man approached holding a bright yellow umbrella. Instead of squeezing beside her, he simply extended the umbrella so it covered them both.

"Looks like we will be here a while," he said pleasantly.

Mira nodded. She was not used to kindness from strangers. The city often felt rushed, distant. The umbrella cast a soft circle of shared space around them, warm and surprising.

They talked about small things. Weather. The delayed bus. The bakery across the street with the line that never seemed to shorten. The minutes stretched, but the wait no longer felt lonely.

When the bus arrived, they boarded together. Mira started to move toward the back, but the man gently stopped her.

"You forgot this," he said, handing her the yellow umbrella.

"Oh, I cannot take that."

"You can. I have another at home."

She hesitated, but his smile was steady. She accepted the umbrella and thanked him. They never exchanged names. She sat down as he found a seat near the front. At the next stop he waved before stepping off into the rain.

The umbrella felt unusually light in her hands.

That evening, Mira dried it carefully and set it by her door. She had not realized how much a simple act could shift her sense of belonging. The city felt different now. Softer. Less distant.

Three days later, she saw another person caught in a sudden rainfall. An exhausted delivery cyclist struggled on the corner, water streaming off his jacket. Without thinking, Mira approached him and held the yellow umbrella over them both.

"Take it," she said. "I insist."

His face lit with surprised gratitude. He accepted it with both hands.

Mira walked home without cover. She did not mind the rain. Something inside her felt brighter than the gray sky above.

That night, she found herself smiling at the memory of the stranger at the bus stop. Hope had arrived disguised as a borrowed umbrella, and she realized that some kindnesses are meant to be passed forward, not kept.

The Garden Behind the Fence

Behind the tall fence on Alder Street was a garden no one could quite see. Vines peeked through the slats, and in summer the scent of basil drifted along the pavement. Children often whispered theories about what grew there. Some imagined exotic plants, others imagined hidden animals. Only one person knew the truth, and she rarely spoke of it.

Mrs. Rivera tended the garden each dawn. She had started it years earlier after losing her husband. The garden became her way of steadying her heart. She planted herbs for comfort, tomatoes for sweetness and wildflowers for surprise. She preferred privacy, not because she wished to hide the garden but because she was shy about its imperfections.

One morning, as she watered the marigolds, she heard a soft sniffle. Through a small gap in the fence, she saw a boy sitting on the curb with his backpack at his feet. His eyes were red.

Mrs. Rivera hesitated, then gently pushed open the side gate. The hinges groaned. The boy looked up, startled.

"Are you hurt?" she asked.

"No," he said. "Just a hard morning."

She nodded. She knew the feeling. She invited him inside, unsure whether he would accept. He followed quietly, wiping his sleeve across his face.

When he stepped into the garden, he froze. Rows of green shimmered with dew. Colorful flowers leaned toward the light. Bees hovered lazily above lavender. Something in the air felt kinder than the street outside.

"It is beautiful," he whispered.

Mrs. Rivera smiled. "This place listens. Plants do not judge."

He walked along a path of stepping stones, touching leaves lightly. His shoulders relaxed. His breathing slowed. After a while, he asked if he could visit again. She said yes without hesitation.

Over the next weeks the boy returned often. He helped prune shrubs and sprinkle seeds. He carried water buckets with surprising determination. Mrs. Rivera watched him grow steadier, calmer. His mother stopped by one afternoon to thank her, explaining that the garden had become a refuge during a difficult time at school.

Word spread quietly. Neighbors brought pots with seedlings to share. A retired carpenter repaired the gate. Students painted a small sign that read: Community Garden. Mrs. Rivera had never planned for company, yet she found she enjoyed it. The garden grew brighter with each new pair of hands.

On the first warm day of spring, the boy brought her a single sapling wrapped in cloth. "For hope," he said.

She planted it carefully beside the fence. As she pressed soil around its roots, she realized the garden had transformed. It had begun as a place to heal alone. Now it had become a place to heal together.

And the young tree, small but determined, seemed to understand exactly what it had been planted to represent.

The Song in the Underpass

The underpass beneath the railway tracks was usually a place people hurried through. The walls were covered in faded graffiti, the lights flickered and the echo of footsteps always felt a little uneasy. Yet each morning at eight, a soft voice filled the tunnel with music.

A street musician named Rowan stood against the center pillar, singing gentle folk melodies that carried through the concrete like threads of warmth. He never opened a case for money. He simply sang. People rarely paused long enough to listen, but they slowed their steps without realising it. The music softened the sharpness of the morning rush.

Elise walked through the underpass every day on her way to work. She had recently been struggling with persistent doubts about her future, small fears that clung to her even when she tried to shake them off. Rowan's voice became the one steady part of her fragile mornings.

One rainy day she finally stopped. Rowan finished a verse and looked up with a surprised smile.

"You have a beautiful voice," Elise said.

"Thank you," he replied. "I sing because someone once sang for me when I needed it."

She hesitated. "Your music helps more than you know."

Rowan nodded, touched. "That is a gift to hear."

The next morning, Elise found a small handwritten sign taped near Rowan's pillar. It read: If these songs bring you comfort, take one with you. Beneath it hung strips of paper, each with a short lyric or thought.

Elise tore one gently. It said: Today can still be kind.

She carried it all day, tucked inside her sleeve. Each time she felt overwhelmed, she touched the paper and breathed a little steadier.

Over the following weeks, she noticed others taking slips as well. A teenager with headphones. A tired nurse. A courier balancing boxes. Rowan continued singing, but now the underpass felt different. Softer. Less forgotten.

One morning Elise arrived to find Rowan missing. Instead, a small speaker sat on the pillar with a note beside it. Work called me early today. Press play if you still need a song.

Elise pressed the button. Rowan's voice filled the tunnel. A few people looked up, surprised, then smiled. Someone else pressed the button again after the track finished.

The underpass did not feel gloomy anymore. It felt like a place where strangers had quietly agreed to take care of one another.

Elise kept the paper slip for months. It eventually faded, but the message stayed bright. Hope did not need to be loud or perfect. It only needed to be shared.

The Sky Written in Chalk

Every weekend, children drew pictures across the pavement outside the community center. Suns with wide grins. Houses with crooked roofs. Stars scattered in bright colors. The drawings vanished each time it rained, only to return stronger the next week.

Amir, a quiet nine year old, rarely joined. He preferred to watch from a distance. His father had been deployed overseas for more than a year, and Amir carried the absence like a heavy coat. His mother tried to keep him cheerful, but some days seemed harder than others.

One Saturday, the chalk boxes were opened early. Volunteers had planned a small festival with music and warm bread. While other children rushed to decorate the pavement, Amir lingered near the wall, hugging his knees.

A volunteer named Grace noticed him and crouched nearby. "Not in the mood to draw today?"

Amir shrugged. "I do not know what to draw."

Grace picked up a piece of pale blue chalk. "You could start with something small. A cloud. A bird. A color you like."

Amir took the chalk reluctantly. He knelt on the pavement and drew a few soft lines. Then he added a sun. Then a hill. Then a tiny figure walking toward the horizon.

"What is he looking for?" Grace asked.

"He is waiting for someone," Amir replied.

The drawing grew. A second figure appeared in the distance. Then a dotted line of footprints connecting the two. Children gathered around, curious. Soon several of them added their own touches. Flowers. Stars. A dog racing across the hill.

One little girl drew a plane in the sky. Amir paused when he saw it. His eyes softened.

"That looks like my father's plane," he whispered.

Grace touched his shoulder gently. "Would you like to draw something for him?"

He nodded. Using bright yellow chalk, he wrote a message near the horizon: Come home soon. I am waiting.

Parents who passed by slowed to read it. A few smiled. A few felt their throats tighten. The picture had become more than pavement art. It carried longing, tenderness and the courage of a child trying to make sense of distance.

Near sunset, Amir's mother arrived and stood still at

the edge of the drawing. She covered her mouth with her hand. "You made this?" she asked.

Amir nodded shyly. "Everyone helped."

She knelt and hugged him tightly. "He would be proud of you."

Rain came late that night and washed away the colors, but the next morning something new appeared at the community center entrance: a photograph of the drawing taped to the door with a note beside it.

It read: Your message was seen. Your hope reached farther than you think.

Amir stood before it for a long while, and in his chest, a small light began to grow again.

The Train Whistle at Evening

Every evening at precisely seven thirty, the train passed behind Lila's apartment building. She had grown used to the sound, a long gentle whistle that stretched across the rooftops. When she first moved in, she found it intrusive. Over time, it became a comfort, a reminder that something steady moved through the world even when her own life felt uncertain.

Lila worked late nights at a small print shop. Winter had been difficult, filled with long shifts and colder days. She sometimes ate dinner alone, listening to the train and wondering what it was like to travel somewhere new instead of staying in place.

One evening, after an exhausting day, she dropped her keys near the stairwell. As she bent to pick them up, she noticed a small envelope tucked between two steps. Someone had written a simple message on the front: For a fellow listener.

Curious, she opened it. Inside was a tiny watercolor painting of the train that passed each night. The colors were soft, mostly blues and purples, with a bright streak of gold along the horizon. On the back of the painting was a note.

"I hear it too," it read. "The whistle reminds me that movement is possible even on days when we feel still."

Lila felt a warmth rise in her chest. She looked around but saw no one. The stairwell was empty, the hallway quiet.

She placed the painting on her kitchen shelf where she could see it while cooking. Each evening, when the whistle echoed across the sky, she glanced at the painting and felt a little steadier.

Months passed. Spring softened the edges of winter. One night Lila found herself humming while closing the shop. She realised she felt different. Not fully changed, but lighter.

That week she bought a set of blank notecards. One afternoon she painted a small scene of her own: a window glowing warmly against a dark street. Beneath it she wrote, "Someone is glad you are here."

She left the card in the stairwell, tucked in the same spot where she had found the envelope. She did not wait for anyone to claim it. That was part of the beauty. Hope did not demand recognition. It simply asked to be passed forward.

When the train whistle sounded that night, Lila stood by her window and listened. The sound no longer felt like a reminder of longing. It felt like a reminder of possibility.

And for the first time in many months, she believed in her own motion again.

The Lighthouse Model

Owen lived in a small attic apartment filled with the soft clutter of a life rebuilt from difficult years. He collected model lighthouses, each no taller than his forearm, arranged neatly on shelves. Some were replicas of real structures, others invented entirely. He said the lights helped him remember that guidance could come from unlikely places.

He often visited the local hobby shop on weekends. One Saturday he found a broken lighthouse model in the clearance bin, missing its railing and chipped along the base. Most customers ignored it. Owen felt drawn to it immediately. He held it carefully, imagining its original shape.

The shop owner shook his head. "That one is beyond repair."

"I think it still has potential," Owen said.

He bought it for a few coins and carried it home in both hands. Repairing models had become a quiet ritual for him. He worked with patience, gluing delicate pieces, sanding rough edges, repainting small details. The broken lighthouse took longer than expected. Some nights he questioned whether it could ever stand straight again.

But slowly, with steady work, it regained its form. He replaced the railing using a thin wire he bent gently. He painted the chipped base and added a new coat of white to the tower. Last, he fitted a tiny bulb inside and tested it. The light flickered once, then glowed steadily.

When he placed it on the windowsill, it looked as though it had always belonged there.

A week later Owen invited his neighbor, Mira, for tea. She had recently moved in after a difficult breakup and often kept to herself. She noticed the lighthouse immediately.

"You restored this?" she asked.

Owen nodded. "It took time, but it was worth it."

She traced the smooth surface with her finger. "It looks perfect."

"Not perfect," he said gently. "Just whole in a new way."

Mira grew quiet, her eyes softening. She seemed to understand the message without needing further explanation.

Over the next months she visited often. They talked late into evenings. She brought pastries. He shared stories about each model, how he found them, what had drawn him in. Their friendship grew not through grand gestures but through the steady comfort of shared space.

One afternoon, Mira brought Owen a gift wrapped in brown paper. Inside was a small unfinished model of a lighthouse.

"I think I am ready to try building one," she said. "Would you show me how?"

Owen felt a warmth bloom inside him. Hope, he realised, was not only the light that guides. Sometimes it is the simple willingness to begin again.

Together they sat at the table, pieces spread out before them, ready to create something new.

The Path of Lantern Leaves

In the park near the river, a path of trees shed bright yellow leaves each autumn. Locals called them lantern leaves because they glowed softly in late afternoon light. During difficult years, people often walked that path for comfort. Something about the warm color lifted spirits.

Callie visited the path every evening after work. She was recovering from a long illness and still felt fragile, as if a strong wind could tip her over. Her doctor had recommended gentle movement, so she walked slowly, counting her steps, breathing in the crisp air.

One evening she noticed a pattern in the leaves. Someone had arranged a handful of them into spirals along the path. Small, deliberate shapes. As she walked farther, she found more spirals, each slightly larger than the last.

At the final tree, a child knelt on the ground, adding a leaf to a spiral that nearly glowed in the fading sun.

"That is beautiful," Callie said softly.

The child looked up. "I like making them. People smile when they see them."

Callie crouched beside her. "Do you make them every day?"

"Most days," the child said. "My dad calls them hope

spirals. He says they remind people that things can grow outward even from small centers."

Callie paused, touched by the idea. She added a leaf of her own. The child beamed.

Over the next week, Callie found herself looking forward to the spirals. Some days they were large and bright, other days tiny and scattered. They became markers of gentle progress, small reminders that creativity did not require strength, only intention.

One late afternoon, she reached the end of the path and saw the child sitting quietly, shoulders slumped. The spirals were missing.

"Are you alright?" Callie asked.

The child nodded but did not smile. "Dad is sick. I wanted to make him a big spiral, but I did not know how."

Callie sat beside her. "Then let us make one together."

They gathered leaves, handfuls at a time. Callie arranged them while the child chose the brightest ones. Slowly, the spiral took shape. Passersby noticed and joined. A couple on a jog. An elderly man with a cane. A teenager carrying her skateboard. Soon the spiral grew larger than any that had come before. The child watched with wide, shining eyes.

When it was complete, Callie handed her the final leaf. The child placed it gently in the center.

"This one is for him," she whispered.

The wind stirred, catching the edges of the leaves. The entire spiral shimmered.

The child turned to Callie. "Thank you."

Callie squeezed her hand. "Hope grows when we make it together."

For the first time in months, Callie felt strong enough to believe it.

The Clockmaker's Promise

The clock shop at the corner of Hemsworth Street was easy to miss. Its windows fogged in winter, and its sign hung slightly crooked. Inside, dozens of clocks ticked softly, none quite in sync. The sound reminded visitors of rainfall.

Mr. Talbot, the clockmaker, was a quiet man with steady hands. He had run the shop for more than forty years. People visited him not only to repair clocks but to hear reassuring words spoken in his calm and patient voice. He never rushed. He never scolded a broken mechanism. He treated time itself as something gentle.

One afternoon a young woman entered the shop holding a small silver watch. It had belonged to her grandmother. The watch had stopped the week before and now refused to tick at all.

Mr. Talbot examined it beneath a warm lamp. "This watch has seen a great deal," he murmured. "There is care worn into every scratch."

"Can it be fixed?" she asked.

The clockmaker hesitated. "The spring is fragile. The gears are tired. It will be difficult, but difficult things are worth trying."

She left it with him and returned home carrying both worry and hope.

For days Mr. Talbot worked in careful intervals. Each time he opened the watch, he felt as though he were holding a memory. He polished each tiny gear. He adjusted the spring until it glimmered faintly. At last he wound it and listened.

Silence.

He closed his eyes, thinking of the grandmother who must have carried it through seasons of laughter and grief. He whispered a small apology to the watch, though no one heard him, and tried again.

A faint tick answered.

When the young woman returned, he placed the restored watch in her hands. She held it to her ear, eyes bright.

"I thought I had lost this part of her," she said quietly.

Mr. Talbot shook his head. "Nothing precious is truly lost. Sometimes it only rests."

She thanked him again and again. After she left, the shop felt lighter, as if the clocks themselves approved of his persistence.

Later that evening he found a small envelope tucked beneath the door. Inside was a note written in gentle handwriting. Thank you for believing in this watch. It meant more than you know.

Mr. Talbot smiled and placed the note beside the lamp. The clocks continued ticking around him in their soft, uneven rhythm. Each tick felt like a reminder that healing often begins in the smallest movements.

He wound his own pocket watch, a gift from his late wife, and listened for its steady beat. It ticked softly in his palm, a quiet promise that time still carried hope.

The Daffodils by the Mailbox

The daffodils beside Marjorie's mailbox bloomed earlier than any others on the street. Neighbors often joked that they were impatient for spring. In truth, Marjorie planted them as a ritual each year to honor her late sister, who had loved bright yellow flowers more than anything.

One winter was particularly harsh. Ice cracked along the pavement. Wind rattled windows. Many people doubted the daffodils would return. Marjorie checked the soil each morning, brushing aside frost with chilled fingers. Nothing.

Her neighbor, Mr. Lyons, watched from his porch. He often saw her stoop beside the mailbox with a hopeful expression that faded a little each day. He wanted to comfort her but never found the right words.

One cold morning he approached her. "I could help reinforce the soil if you want. Maybe add warmer mulch."

Marjorie smiled weakly. "Thank you. I planted them for my sister. It feels as if she visits when they bloom."

Together they knelt in the cold. Mr. Lyons added mulch while Marjorie whispered stories about her sister. They laughed softly at shared memories. For the first time since winter began, Marjorie felt warmth in the act.

Weeks passed. The frost thinned. Birds returned cautiously. One afternoon Marjorie stepped outside and gasped. A single green sprout pushed through the soil. Tiny. Trembling. Alive.

She called to Mr. Lyons. He hurried over with a grin. "Looks like they were only hiding."

The next day two more appeared. Then five. Then a cluster. By the end of the week the daffodils stood bright and proud, their yellow petals catching sunlight like small lanterns.

Neighbors paused when they walked by. Some left handwritten notes of encouragement in Marjorie's mailbox. Children took pictures. One woman placed a small ribbon near the blooms.

Marjorie felt something inside her soften. Her grief had grown heavy during the dark months, but seeing the flowers returned her to herself. They were not just blooms. They were reminders. Persistence can rise from frozen ground. Love can grow again.

On the first warm evening of spring, Marjorie and Mr. Lyons sat on her porch sipping tea while the daffodils swayed in gentle wind.

"Thank you for helping me," she said quietly.

Mr. Lyons shook his head. "You kept faith in them long before I arrived."

Marjorie smiled. "Even so. It feels easier to hope with someone beside you."

The daffodils glowed in the fading light. And for the first time in months, Marjorie felt her sister's memory settle not as a weight but as a comfort.

The Sparrow on Elm Road

When the power outage swept across the neighborhood, people gathered outside their houses, blinking up at the sudden darkness. With streetlights off, the area looked unfamiliar. Children clung to parents. Adults murmured about when electricity might return.

Eliza stepped onto her porch with a blanket around her shoulders. She had been feeling disconnected from her community since moving in, convinced everyone else already belonged while she remained an outsider.

Then she noticed something unusual. A small sparrow perched on a fallen branch near the curb. It chirped loudly, unfazed by the crowd or the darkness. The sound was bright and determined, as if the sparrow was claiming the night as its own.

A child pointed. "Why is it singing now?"

"Maybe it thinks the stars are watching," her father said.

Eliza laughed softly. A few neighbors glanced toward her with friendly expressions. She felt a slight shift, like a door opening.

The sparrow hopped toward a puddle reflecting the faint glow of the sky. It splashed, sending tiny ripples outward. The simple joy of it was contagious. People began stepping closer, forming a loose circle around the bird.

An elderly woman whispered, "Maybe it is telling us not to worry."

A man added, "Maybe it enjoys the quiet."

Someone suggested placing seeds near the branch. Another person fetched a small dish of water. Eliza gathered crumbs from a bag of crackers she had been carrying and sprinkled them gently.

The sparrow chirped again. Its voice rang like a bright thread of sound through the stillness. For a moment everyone forgot the outage. They simply stood together, sharing a moment shaped by a creature smaller than any of them.

A teenager turned on her phone flashlight and pointed it toward the ground. The light illuminated the sparrow in a soft glow. It fluttered its wings, lifted briefly into the air, then landed on the branch once more. The child who had spoken earlier clapped in delight.

When the electricity returned twenty minutes later, the sudden brightness surprised everyone. The spell broke, yet something remained. People began talking to one another. Introductions were exchanged. Laughter spread across the street.

Eliza found herself chatting with the elderly woman, who lived two houses down. They discovered they both loved gardening and arranged to exchange seeds in the spring.

As the crowd dispersed, the sparrow took flight, vanishing into the night as quietly as it had arrived.

Inside her home, Eliza felt lighter. The neighborhood no longer seemed like a place she had entered too late. It felt like a place she could grow into. She closed her curtains gently, thinking of the sparrow's bright call cutting through darkness.

Hope, she realized, often comes from voices that refuse to quiet themselves.

The Constellation Quilt

Nadia had inherited a box of fabric squares from her grandmother, each one patterned with stars. Some were dark indigo, some pale silver, others dotted with tiny constellations drawn in white thread. Her grandmother had planned to make a quilt but never finished it.

For years the box sat untouched in Nadia's closet. She had always wanted to sew but felt too intimidated to begin. Her grandmother had been a master quilter with steady hands and a patient spirit. Nadia feared she would dishonor the memory by doing it badly.

One winter evening, during a stretch of nights that felt heavy and isolating, she opened the box and spread the squares across her living room floor. The patterns formed a scattered sky beneath her feet. Something in her chest stirred.

She threaded a needle with shaking hands and began stitching two pieces together. The seam was uneven. The fabric puckered slightly. She sighed but continued.

Over the next days she worked slowly, sometimes for only ten minutes, sometimes for hours. She sat by the window where lamplight softened the imperfections. The quilt began to grow. The shapes aligned into constellations of her own making.

Neighbors noticed the soft glow of her lamp each evening. One night her upstairs neighbor, Ms. Lee, knocked and asked if she could help. She had sewn for years and missed the company of shared projects. Nadia welcomed her in.

They worked side by side, stitching, talking, sipping tea. Ms. Lee never corrected Nadia's technique harshly. She simply guided with gentle suggestions. As the quilt grew, more neighbors joined. A retired teacher. A young couple. A teenager learning embroidery. Soon the quilt became a collaborative effort filled with the warmth of many hands.

When the final stitch was placed, Nadia spread the quilt across her bed. The stars shimmered softly against the dark fabric, like a night sky pulled gently indoors. She felt tears prick her eyes.

Ms. Lee placed a hand on her shoulder. "Your grandmother would be proud."

"It is full of mistakes," Nadia whispered.

"All quilts are," Ms. Lee said. "The beauty is in the care, not the perfection."

Word spread quickly. The community center invited Nadia to display the quilt for a weekend showcase. Visitors admired the constellations, tracing the seams that joined pieces of many lives. Nadia stood quietly in the background, watching strangers appreciate something she once feared to begin.

When she returned home that evening, she wrapped the quilt around her shoulders. The weight felt comforting. Not heavy. Steady.

She looked at the night sky through her window and felt a connection between the stars above and the stars sewn into fabric.

Hope, she realized, was simply a constellation that people build together, one small stitch at a time.

The Door Painted Sunrise

The abandoned house on Willow Lane had been empty for years. Children rode their bikes past it without stopping. Adults avoided it on late walks. Its chipped paint and cracked windows made it seem beyond saving.

Then one Saturday morning, the neighborhood woke to find the front door painted in radiant colors. Pink, orange and gold blended into a soft gradient that resembled sunrise. A small sign hung beside it that read: Work in progress. Please keep hope.

Curiosity spread. Who had painted it? Why only the door?

The following week, a young artist named Tamsin appeared with a ladder and several buckets of paint. She lived three streets away and had recently lost her job. She wanted something to occupy her hands and steady her mind. While passing the abandoned house, she felt a pull she could not explain.

"I wanted to give the street something bright," she told anyone who asked. "Something that says things can change."

She worked quietly. Each day she painted a little more. A patch of sky. A field of soft green. Delicate vines curling around the porch posts. Children gathered to watch. Some offered to help. Parents brought her lemonade and sandwiches. A retired handyman repaired a loose shutter.

The house transformed slowly. People stopped avoiding it and began stopping to admire it instead. Even those who disliked bright colors found themselves smiling.

One afternoon, while painting a cluster of flowers near the windowsill, Tamsin slipped from the ladder. A neighbor rushed forward to catch her. She laughed shakily. "Maybe I needed a reminder that not everything must be done alone."

Her work continued, steadier now with more assistance. A high school art class volunteered to paint the side panels. A local carpenter rebuilt the front steps. Within a month the house no longer looked abandoned. It looked hopeful, alive, waiting.

When the final brushstroke dried, the whole neighborhood gathered for an informal unveiling. The house stood bright against the street, covered in sunrise colors and painted gardens. Tamsin stepped back, paint still smudging her hands.

A child tugged her sleeve. "Is it finished?"

Tamsin looked at the house, then at the people around her. "I think the house is finished," she said. "But hope never is."

The neighbors agreed to maintain the property together until the city decided on its future. Some wanted to turn it into a community center. Others suggested a public art space. What mattered most was that it no longer stood as a symbol of neglect.

As Tamsin walked home that night, she glanced over her shoulder. The door glowed softly in the fading light, warm as a promise.

She felt something rising inside her, gentle and strong. A reminder that even when life feels stalled, a single stroke of color can invite change.

Chapter 2

WINTER MAGIC

In the hush of cold air
and early falling light,
the ordinary world lifts its veil
for anyone who still believes in wonder.

The Snowfall That Forgot to Stop

The snow began just after dawn, soft flakes drifting in
slow spirals. Mara watched from her apartment
window while sipping tea. She expected the storm to
pass quickly. Instead, the snow deepened, quieting
the world until even the usual Sunday traffic seemed
to vanish.

By afternoon, the snowfall took on a peculiar glow.
Each flake sparkled faintly as if catching light from an
unseen source. Children hurried outside to twirl

beneath it, laughing as the air shimmered around them. Mara hesitated before joining them, wrapping herself in her wool coat and stepping carefully into the brightness.

The snowflakes landed on her sleeves with a delicate sparkle, refusing to melt immediately. She held out her hand, mesmerized. The flakes stayed whole long enough for her to see patterns she had never imagined tiny spirals, miniature stars, delicate lattices. A little girl beside her gasped.

"They look alive," the girl whispered.

Mara nodded. The air felt charged with possibility. She noticed that each person who stepped into the snow seemed to fall quiet for a moment as if listening for something hidden within the falling light.

As evening approached, the snowfall finally softened. Neighbors lingered outside, reluctant to return indoors. Someone remarked that the world seemed gentler. Someone else said it felt like standing inside a dream.

Mara returned to her apartment and brushed the lingering flakes from her coat. A single flake refused to fall away. It rested on her sleeve, still glowing faintly, still perfectly intact. She held it close and whispered a wish without knowing why.

The flake shimmered once, then melted into her palm.

The next morning the snowfall was gone. Streets were clear, sidewalks swept, rooftops bare. Yet people spoke about the previous day in hushed tones, as if uncertain whether it had truly happened.

Mara opened her curtains and noticed something small on her windowsill. A tiny crystal shape, resembling the glowing flakes, sat there shining gently in the morning light.

She smiled. Winter, she understood, had decided to leave her a reminder that wonder does not always vanish when the storm ends.

Midnight at the Frozen Pond

Every winter, the pond behind the old school froze solid enough for skating. Families visited during the day, but at night the place belonged to anyone brave enough to wander out beneath the stars.

Theo preferred the late hours. He found comfort in the way moonlight brushed the ice with silver. One particularly cold night, he walked to the pond wrapped in a thick scarf. The sky was clear, and the world felt quiet enough to hear his own breath.

As he stepped onto the ice, he heard music. Soft, distant, lilting. It sounded like a violin played from somewhere across the pond. Theo paused, heart thudding with curiosity.

A figure soon appeared on the opposite side. A woman stood poised with a violin tucked beneath her chin. Her bow glided effortlessly. The melody floated through the night like gentle wind.

Theo approached slowly. The ice beneath him glimmered. As he drew near, the woman lowered her bow.

"I thought I was alone," she said.

"So did I."

They stood in silence for a moment before she began playing again, this time a slower tune that echoed beautifully in the night air. Theo felt warmth rise through him despite the cold.

"You play for the pond?" he asked when the piece ended.

She smiled. "For the quiet. For anyone who needs to remember that stillness can be beautiful."

He nodded, understanding more than he could explain.

Before leaving, she reached into her coat and offered him a small folded card. Inside was a short note. When winter feels heavy, listen for what shines in the quiet.

Theo looked up to thank her, but she had already skated away, her figure fading into moonlit distance.

From that night onward, he returned to the pond whenever life felt too heavy. Some nights he heard the violin, soft and distant. Other nights he heard only the whisper of wind across the ice. Both brought comfort.

Winter, he realized, carries its own kind of music. You simply have to step outside to hear it.

The Candle in the Window

During the coldest week of the year, the apartments on Maple Lane seemed deserted. Curtains remained closed. People hurried indoors. Winter had tightened its grip, and the neighborhood felt subdued.

But one window stood out. A single candle glowed warmly each evening in the third floor corner apartment. Its flame flickered in steady rhythm, casting soft shapes on the frosted glass.

Claire passed it each night on her walk home from work. The candle intrigued her. Though small, it radiated something comforting. She began timing her walk so she could pause beneath the window for a moment.

One night she saw someone adjusting the candle. A man with gentle features leaned forward, checking the wick. Claire felt a strange impulse and raised her hand in greeting. To her surprise, he smiled and waved back.

The next evening, a small paper heart appeared in the window. Beneath it someone had written, Keep warm.

Claire felt her cheeks warm despite the cold. She wrote her own message on a slip of paper and held it up toward the window. Thank you for the light.

The man nodded and lifted his candle slightly as if offering it to her.

This quiet exchange continued for days. Sometimes the man placed tiny cutouts in the window. Snowflakes. Stars. One night a small paper fox. Claire responded with drawings of her own.

One evening when snow fell harder than expected, Claire slipped on the ice near the building. The candle flickered out for a moment as she steadied herself. Before she could rise, the man appeared at the door offering a gloved hand.

"You must be Claire," he said. "I recognize the drawings."

She laughed softly. "And you must be the candle keeper."

He walked her home, brushing snow from her coat as they went. When they reached her door he said, "I light the candle for my sister. She passed away last winter. Keeping it glowing helps me remember warmth still exists."

Claire touched his arm gently. "It does."

They parted with a quiet understanding that winter had brought them together.

The next night, two candles glowed side by side in his window. A soft reminder that shared light shines brighter.

The Visitor in the Snowstorm

When the storm hit, it arrived with sudden force. Nora had expected flurries, not a white curtain of swirling snow that erased the world beyond her porch. She wrapped herself in blankets and resigned herself to a long evening alone.

Near midnight she heard a faint tapping on her door. She startled, wondering who would be out in such weather. When she opened the door, a husky stood on her porch, fur dusted with snow, eyes bright and expectant.

Nora hesitated. "Where did you come from?"

The dog wagged its tail and stepped forward, seeking warmth. She let it inside and wiped snow from its fur. Its collar held no tag, only a silver charm shaped like a crescent moon.

The husky lay near the fireplace, sighing contentedly. Nora sat beside it, feeling a strange sense of company. The storm outside roared, but the room felt protected, almost enchanted.

Hours passed. The dog remained calm, watching her with intelligent eyes. She spoke to it quietly about her week, her loneliness, her wish for winter to feel less isolating. The husky listened as though understanding every word.

Near dawn, the storm faded. Light filtered through the windows. Nora opened the door to check the porch. A man approached from the direction of the woods.

"That is my companion," he said kindly. "Her name is Luna. She wanders ahead of me sometimes."

Nora scratched the dog's ears. "She kept me safe last night."

"She does that," he replied. "She finds people who need company."

Before leaving, he handed Nora the moon charm from Luna's collar. "Keep this. A small token of gratitude."

Nora watched them disappear into the snowy path. The charm felt warm in her hand despite the cold air.

From that morning onward, winter felt different. The storm had brought a visitor. And the memory of a loyal dog who arrived precisely when she needed a reminder that no one is truly alone.

The Maple Street Snow Globe

The antique shop at the corner sold odd items: cracked teacups, forgotten postcards, warped records.

But the most curious object was a snow globe perched near the register. It showed a tiny perfect street with small houses, a bakery and a lamppost glowing faintly.

Amelia visited the shop every week. She always paused at the snow globe. The miniature world inside looked strangely familiar, though she could not place why.

One icy afternoon, she finally asked the shopkeeper, "Where did this come from?"

He shrugged. "It arrived anonymously. People either ignore it or cannot stop looking at it."

Amelia lifted the snow globe. When she shook it gently, snowflakes swirled and settled in slow patterns. The lamppost flickered softly.

That night she dreamed of walking down a quiet street that looked exactly like the miniature neighborhood. In the dream she passed a bakery with warm light and heard distant laughter.

The next day she returned to the shop. The snow globe glowed slightly brighter. Amelia frowned. "Was it always this bright?"

The shopkeeper squinted. "Hard to say. Winter light plays tricks."

With each visit, the snow globe seemed to reflect her mood. When she felt lonely, the lamppost shone more warmly. When she felt hopeful, the snow sparkled brighter. She began keeping a journal of these small changes.

One morning she hurried into the shop, breathless from excitement. Overnight it had snowed heavily, and the street outside looked identical to the street inside the globe. She lifted the snow globe and shook it gently. The flakes swirled. The lamppost glowed.

"It is as if it wants to show you something," the shopkeeper said softly.

Amelia stepped outside and followed her instincts. She walked along Maple Street, past the bakery she always ignored, past houses she had never truly seen.

At the end of the street, she found a small park with a single bench covered in snow. She sat down and waited, unsure why.

Moments later, a woman holding a dog approached. She paused. "I have been meaning to speak with you. You live near here, do you not?"

Amelia nodded. Something warm moved inside her chest.

The woman smiled. "I often see you walking alone. I thought you might enjoy company next time."

Amelia returned the smile. "I would."

That night the snow globe glowed softly on her shelf, brighter than ever. The world inside it no longer felt mysterious. It felt like a reminder to step into her own life with more attention and more courage.

And the next morning, the lamppost inside the globe flickered in greeting.

The Cold Air Orchard

The orchard on Hillcrest Road was known for its apples in autumn, but few people visited it during winter. Most assumed the trees slept beneath frost, offering nothing of interest.

Larkin thought otherwise. He walked there each winter morning to breathe the cold air that carried the faint scent of bark and distant sweetness. The orchard always felt quiet yet alive.

One morning, he noticed something strange. A tree near the center glowed faintly beneath the frost. Its branches shimmered with tiny crystals that caught the pale sunlight in unusual colors.

As he approached, he heard a soft ringing sound. Not a bell, not metal, something closer to wind harmonies. The glow intensified.

A woman stood on the far side of the tree, equally surprised. "You see it too," she said.

Larkin nodded. "I thought I was imagining the sound."

"No. It only happens on the coldest mornings." She reached out and touched a branch lightly. The crystals vibrated, sending gentle ripples of color through the air.

They marveled at the sight together. She introduced herself as Rowan. She walked the orchard to clear her thoughts after long nights of caring for her aging father. Larkin admitted he came for peace during a difficult transition in his own life.

The glowing tree felt like a bridge between their quiet struggles.

They began meeting at the orchard each morning. Some days the tree glowed, some days it did not. What mattered was the shared quiet. They spoke gently about their lives, their hopes, their weariness. The winter air felt kinder when shared.

One morning, the glow was brighter than ever, casting soft blue light over the snow. Rowan closed her eyes and whispered, "It feels like the tree is singing."

Larkin listened and felt the same.

A week later the frost melted and the orchard lost its winter crystals. Yet the connection between Larkin and Rowan remained. They continued walking the orchard even when branches grew bare and ordinary.

Winter magic does not last forever, but sometimes it lingers long enough to show people what can grow in its place.

And in that orchard, beneath the tree that once glowed, something steady and hopeful had begun.

The Bakery with the Frosted Window

Each winter the bakery on Sycamore Street decorated its windows with intricate frost patterns. They appeared naturally, but always in shapes that seemed too artful to be random. Spirals. Ferns. Feathers. Wings.

Lina visited the bakery daily for a warm pastry. She often paused outside to admire the frost before entering. The patterns seemed to change subtly each morning, as if they were leaving quiet messages only she could read.

One day, she noticed a small heart shape in the frost near the corner of the glass. She leaned closer. The heart pointed toward a spot inside the bakery where chairs sat empty.

She took her usual place, but her gaze kept drifting toward the indicated seat. Moments later, a man entered carrying a sketchbook. He chose the very chair the frost heart had pointed to.

He opened the sketchbook and began drawing the frost on the window. Lina watched, intrigued by the deliberate strokes.

When he noticed her looking, he smiled. "It is like the window is alive."

"I have always thought that," she replied.

They began talking about the patterns. He introduced himself as Oliver, a winter enthusiast who wandered the city searching for beautiful cold weather phenomena. Lina admitted she loved the bakery window more than she loved most pastries.

The frost seemed to listen. The next morning, a new pattern emerged. Two spirals intertwined. Lina smiled, feeling as though the window approved of their meeting.

Oliver returned daily. They discussed art, books, weather oddities and pastries. Winter felt lighter with his presence.

One evening the frost melted completely during an unexpected warm spell. The window stood plain and transparent. Lina felt oddly sad.

Oliver arrived and touched the clear glass. "It only means new patterns will return," he said. "Magic rests but it does not disappear."

Lina nodded. She reached for his hand. "Will you keep coming even without the frost?"

"Of course."

The next morning a fresh frost appeared. This time the pattern resembled two cups side by side, steam curling upward.

Lina laughed. Winter had spoken again. And this time its message was unmistakably warm.

The Lantern Fox

During the winter festival each year, small lanterns were placed along the riverbank. They flickered in shimmering lines that reflected on the icy water.

One year, Mira walked the river path alone. She had recently moved to the town and felt unanchored. The lanterns comforted her, but loneliness followed her like a shadow.

As she paused beside a particularly bright lantern, she noticed movement near the reeds. A fox emerged, its fur pale as snow, its eyes glowing with soft golden light.

The fox stepped closer, unafraid. A faint warmth radiated from it. Mira crouched instinctively.

The fox circled her, then continued along the lantern path. It paused every few steps, glancing back as if inviting her to follow.

Mira did.

The fox led her past the festival crowds to a quiet clearing where lanterns hung from tree branches, swaying gently. The air felt calm and bright, almost otherworldly.

When she reached the clearing, the fox sat beside a tree and looked up at her. For a moment, Mira felt seen in a way she had not felt seen in months.

"Thank you," she whispered.

The fox blinked slowly, then turned and trotted back toward the reeds. It vanished among the shadows.

Mira returned to the festival with a lighter heart. She stopped at a booth to buy a warm drink and struck up a conversation with a woman beside her. They chatted easily. The evening felt different, warmer, more welcoming.

The next year Mira returned to the festival and searched quietly for the fox. She never saw it again, but she always left a lantern near the reeds just in case.

Some magic visits only once. Some magic stays in the memory, guiding the heart long after the lanterns fade.

The Frost Kissed Letters

Each winter morning, snow gathered lightly on the street of Old Pine Lane, coating the mailboxes in a shimmering layer of frost. Residents brushed it away without much thought, except for Ruth, who loved the tiny crystals.

One morning she noticed small patterns forming on her mailbox. Letters. Shapes. It looked almost like handwriting drawn in frost.

Curious, she traced the shape with her gloved finger. The frost evaporated instantly but left an impression in her heart. The next morning, new symbols appeared. Little curls. A tiny heart. A star.

Ruth began leaving brief notes inside her mailbox, unsure who might find them. Simple messages. Thank you for the art. Your frost makes my mornings brighter.

The next day, the frost returned, shaped like a smiling face.

Ruth laughed out loud.

This continued for several weeks. Her mailbox became a conversation in frost and ink. Some days the symbols were playful, other days thoughtful. She responded with encouragement, gratitude and tiny sketches.

One snowy morning she found a handwritten letter inside.

"Dear Ruth. I am your neighbor across the street. My daughter has been creating frost art each morning before school. Your notes made winter more joyful for her and for me. Thank you for seeing her magic."

Ruth looked up to see a little girl waving shyly from her porch. Ruth waved back enthusiastically.

The next morning, the frost letters spelled a simple message: Good morning friend.

Ruth placed her palm on the cold mailbox and smiled.

Winter had found a way to speak. And she had learned to listen.

The Wishing Steps

At the edge of town, the old stone staircase led up a small hill overlooking the frozen lake. During summer it was a popular place to rest, but in winter it stood empty, coated in snow.

Legend said the steps granted one small wish each winter to those who climbed them alone at dusk. Most people laughed at the tale. Yet each year a few curious souls visited.

Leah decided to try it on a particularly quiet evening. She had carried a wish in her heart for months, something tender she never spoke aloud.

She reached the bottom step and placed her hand on the cold stone. The air felt still. She climbed slowly, counting each step, her breath forming pale clouds.

At the top she paused. The frozen lake stretched out, reflecting the soft glow of the setting sun. She whispered her wish into the cold air. Not loudly. Just enough for winter to hear.

Nothing happened.

She felt foolish and turned to leave, but then a faint sound reached her ears. A soft ringing, like delicate glass chimes. She looked around but saw nothing.

As she descended the steps, she noticed a shape resting on the final stair. A small white feather. It glowed faintly in the fading light.

She picked it up and felt warmth spread through her palm.

The next morning she received a letter she had been waiting for since autumn, one that confirmed a long hoped for opportunity. Her wish was not granted in the dramatic way she had imagined, yet something gentle had shifted.

Leah returned to the wishing steps often after that. Not to wish again, but to stand at the top and breathe the cold air, letting winter remind her that belief itself is a doorway.

And for her, that was enough.

The Door That Opened to Snowlight

The hallway light in Iris's apartment building often flickered during storms, but she never thought much of It. One evening, after a long shift, she trudged upstairs with grocery bags in her arms. The corridor felt unusually quiet. When she reached her door, she noticed something strange. A pale glow seeped from beneath the frame.

She frowned. She had certainly turned off all her lights that morning.

With cautious curiosity, she unlocked the door. Instead of her dim living room, she saw a gentle landscape of swirling snowlight. Her rug and sofa were still there, but the air shimmered with a faint silver mist, like a dream settling into her home.

She stepped inside. The temperature was cool yet pleasant. The glow radiated from the far wall where light gathered in shifting patterns. It reminded her of moonlit snowfall, but softer and somehow alive.

As she moved closer, the light coalesced into a shape. Not human. Something like a drifting veil of winter. Iris felt no fear. The presence felt warm despite its cold appearance.

A whisper, soft as falling snow, brushed her thoughts. Rest.

Iris's shoulders loosened. She had been holding tension for months. She sank onto the sofa and felt the light pulse gently, as if offering comfort. The glow brightened, then slowly faded.

When the room returned to normal, Iris sat in quiet wonder. The groceries remained untouched on the counter. The flickering hallway light outside hummed normally.

In the days that followed, she found herself feeling steadier, calmer. The memory of the snowlight lingered as a companion in her mind.

She never saw the glow again, but on winter nights she sometimes caught a faint shimmer near the wall. Like a soft reminder that even in exhaustion, something gentle had chosen to meet her.

The Silent Sleigh

The forest trail near Finn's cabin was rarely traveled in winter. Heavy snow made it difficult to navigate, yet he enjoyed the solitude. One cold morning, he ventured out with his thermos of tea and a scarf wrapped snugly around his neck.

As he reached a clearing, he froze. A small sleigh rested near the tree line. Not a modern one, but something old fashioned with wooden runners and silver trim. No tracks led to it or away from it. The sleigh simply sat there, as though waiting.

Finn approached cautiously. The air felt crisp and still. He touched the sleigh. The wood was warm.

A faint bell chimed nearby. Finn spun around, but the forest remained empty.

He placed a hand on the sleigh again and felt an odd sensation, like stepping into a memory. In his mind he saw winter nights from his childhood. His father pulling him on a small sled. Laughter rising into the cold air. The warmth of those moments spread through him.

When he opened his eyes, the sleigh glimmered with soft silver light. He felt an invitation rather than a command.

He sat down.

The sleigh moved gently forward, gliding across the snow with no visible force. Finn did not feel fear. Only wonder. It carried him through the clearing, past the trees, along a path he used to walk as a boy. The forest glowed with a delicate sheen.

After a short, peaceful journey, the sleigh slowed and stopped exactly where he had first found it. The bell chimed once more.

Finn stepped out. The sleigh dimmed, then vanished like mist.

He stood alone in the clearing, but his heart felt full. Winter had returned a piece of himself he thought long gone.

The next morning he walked the trail again. No sleigh. No tracks. Yet the forest felt brighter, as if aware of his gratitude.

Finn never spoke of the sleigh, but every winter he brought a small silver bell to the clearing and hung it on a branch. It chimed softly in the cold air, a memory made real again.

The Snowbound Post Office

During the heaviest storm of the year, the tiny post office on Birch Road remained open. Mail could not leave the building, but people gathered inside for warmth. The old radiator clattered. Snow piled against the door.

Lena worked the counter that day. She enjoyed the quiet. The storm muted the world, turning the post office into a small shelter of shared breath and soft greetings.

A little girl entered carrying a letter sealed in blue wax. Her cheeks were red from the cold. She approached Lena with solemn determination.

"I need this delivered today," the girl said.

Lena smiled kindly. "Nothing will move until the storm passes. But I can hold it safely for you."

The girl hesitated, clutching the envelope. "It is for my grandmother," she whispered. "She passed away last month."

Lena felt a tug in her chest. "Would you like the letter to be kept somewhere special?"

The girl nodded.

Lena led her to a small wooden drawer at the back of the office. "Important letters go here," she said. "Ones that do not need roads or trucks to reach their destination."

The girl placed the envelope inside with great care. "Do you think she will know?"

Lena met her eyes gently. "I believe she already does."

They returned to the front, and the girl lingered until her father arrived to walk her home.

When evening approached, the storm intensified. The lights flickered. Lena locked the doors and sat by the radiator. She thought of the blue wax seal and the tenderness inside that drawer.

As night deepened, she heard faint footsteps. Startled, she looked up. A shape blurred by falling snow stood just outside the window. A soft glow outlined the figure.

The lights steadied. The shape lifted a hand, as though offering thanks. Then it faded gently into the storm.

The next morning the storm ended. The sky was clear. Lena hurried to the drawer. The blue wax envelope remained, but the seal had softened, as though warmed by unseen hands.

When the little girl returned weeks later, Lena gave her the envelope.

"It looks different," the girl murmured.

"Some letters travel in their own way," Lena replied.

The girl pressed the envelope to her heart and smiled softly.

The post office never felt ordinary to Lena again. Each winter she left a candle burning near the drawer, a quiet reminder that love finds its path even through storms.

The Icicle Garden

Behind the greenhouse on Alder Farm, icicles formed along a wooden fence every winter. They were ordinary at first glance, but one year people noticed something peculiar. The icicles seemed to grow in elegant patterns like glass flowers blooming in the cold.

Holly, who worked part time at the farm, was the first to notice. She arrived early one morning to find the icicles shaped like delicate bells and spirals. When the sun hit them, they glowed in pale colors.

She called her coworker Ben to look. He approached skeptically, then froze. "They look alive."

Each day new shapes appeared. Towers, petals, small arches. People from nearby towns began visiting, calling it the Icicle Garden.

Holly felt protective of it. She cleared snow from the fence. She whispered thanks to the cold air. She felt the garden responded, the icicles growing more intricate on days when she arrived with gratitude rather than hurry.

One evening, after a difficult shift, Holly walked to the fence feeling heavy and tired. The garden stood silent. The icicles were plain, almost ordinary.

She sighed and rested her forehead against the wood. "I am trying," she whispered.

A soft crackling sound followed. Holly stepped back. Before her eyes, the icicles began shifting. Within seconds they grew into shapes more delicate than any she had seen. Small flowers unfurled. Tiny towers rose. The fence shimmered.

Ben approached from behind, breath catching. "It listens to you."

Holly touched one of the glass flowers lightly. A warm sensation moved through her fingertips.

The next morning, the Icicle Garden had returned to its usual form. Visitors admired it, unaware of the moment shared the night before.

Holly understood that the magic was not meant to be captured or displayed. It was a conversation between winter and anyone who approached with an open heart.

And each year when the cold returned, Holly walked to the fence first thing, whispering a quiet greeting into the glittering air.

The Winter Letterbox

On the edge of the village stood a peculiar letterbox made entirely of stone. It had no slot, yet every winter people found letters inside it. No one knew who placed them there or how they arrived.

These letters contained short messages of encouragement. Some were anonymous, others signed with simple initials. People called it the Winter Letterbox, believing it appeared only during the coldest months.

Evan discovered it by accident one snowy evening. The lid sat slightly open, revealing a folded note inside.

Curiosity urged him forward.

The note read, You are stronger than you think.

Evan felt his breath catch. He had been struggling silently for months. This message felt impossibly timely.

The next day he returned. Another letter waited. This one said, The world is softer when you look for its kindness.

Evan visited daily. The notes became a source of warmth, reminding him that even unseen hands could offer support.

One morning, he found a woman standing beside the

stone box. She looked startled, then smiled shyly. "I thought I was the only one who came here."

They introduced themselves. Her name was Mara. She had been reading the winter letters for years.

"Do you know who writes them?" Evan asked.

Mara shook her head. "I think winter does. Or maybe people who understand what cold seasons feel like."

They laughed quietly. A gentle bond formed between them.

Late that season, Evan opened the letterbox to find two envelopes. One addressed to him. One addressed to Mara.

His read, Invite someone in. It helps both of you.

Mara's read, Let someone share the warmth you carry.

They stood side by side, holding their letters, understanding the message completely.

From then on, they visited the letterbox together. Spring arrived soon after, and the stone box vanished without explanation.

But the friendship it shaped remained.

The Snowbound Choir

The community choir met every Saturday, even during cold months. Most members walked from nearby homes, carrying music folders and wearing heavy boots. Their rehearsal room was small but warm.

One winter storm arrived so suddenly that only five members made it. The director almost cancelled, but the group insisted they stay awhile to wait out the worst of it.

As the wind howled outside, the lights flickered. The room fell into deep quiet. Someone hummed a melody. Another joined. Soon they were singing softly in harmony, their voices rising and falling like gentle waves.

The storm raged, but the room felt safe. Their song filled the walls, warm and bright. At one point the ceiling lights dimmed completely, yet the group continued singing in the dark.

When the final note faded, something extraordinary happened. The air shimmered with a faint glow, as if the music had gathered into visible warmth. The singers stood still, breath held in wonder.

The director whispered, "I think winter heard us."

The lights returned. The storm eased. The glow faded slowly, leaving behind a sense of calm that lingered long after the group dispersed.

From that night onward, the choir sang differently. Not louder. Not more perfectly. But with a quiet reverence that acknowledged the magic they had shared.

And each winter storm after that felt a little kinder.

The White Owl's Path

Mila walked the forest trail near her grandmother's cottage each winter. The path wound through tall pines and opened to a small meadow. She visited the meadow every season in hopes of spotting the white owl locals spoke about.

One twilight she heard wings above. A large snowy owl settled on a low branch, watching her with calm golden eyes. Mila froze in awe.

The owl blinked slowly, then glided off the branch and landed a short distance down the trail. It looked back at her as if waiting.

Mila followed.

The owl led her through the trees until they reached a narrow clearing she had never seen. The snow there shimmered as though lit from beneath. A gentle breeze whispered through the branches.

Mila felt a strange comfort. She sat on a fallen log and breathed deeply. The owl perched nearby, quiet and majestic.

As she sat in the glow, memories of the past year drifted through her mind. Moments of worry. Loss. Change. Yet here, in this clearing, everything felt held in gentle balance.

She closed her eyes for only a moment. When she opened them, the owl had flown. But a single white feather lay in the snow beside her.

She carried the feather home, placing it on her grandmother's mantel. Her grandmother smiled knowingly.

"Not everyone sees the owl," she said. "It comes to those who need guidance."

Mila touched the feather gently. "It felt like a blessing."

"Maybe it was."

Each winter afterward, Mila walked the trail. She did not always see the owl, yet the clearing seemed easier to find. A soft reminder remained in the shape of that single feather, glowing faintly in her memory.

The Frozen Timepiece

In the small museum at the edge of town, a strange exhibit appeared each winter. A clock encased in clear ice. No plaque explained its origin. No one knew who delivered it. The museum staff found it outside the door every December.

The clock always ticked steadily despite being frozen.

Visitors called it the Frozen Timepiece. Some believed it held protective magic. Others thought it was an elaborate prank.

Carla, a museum volunteer, felt drawn to it. She visited each morning to listen to its soft ticking. On stressful days, the steady sound calmed her.

One evening she stayed after closing to finish paperwork. The museum was quiet. Snow fell gently outside. As Carla passed the clock, the ice shimmered with soft blue light.

She paused. "Are you trying to tell me something?" she whispered.

The ticking slowed, then quickened, almost like a heartbeat. The ice began to melt slightly, revealing intricate engravings beneath the glass surface. She leaned in.

The engraving read, Time does not freeze, but hearts sometimes do. Warmth returns when you let the world in.

Carla felt tears prick her eyes. She had been distant from friends for months, retreating into isolation without meaning to. The message felt impossibly personal.

The light faded. The clock returned to stillness.

By morning the ice had fully refrozen, hiding the engraving again. Carla never spoke of what she saw, but she began reaching out to people she had drifted from.

The museum staff found the clock missing in early

March. No ice. No trace. It always vanished after winter.

Carla felt grateful. Some magic appears only long enough to thaw what needs thawing.

The Night of the Silver Trails

Every few years, on a night known to locals as Winter's Crossing, thin silver trails appeared across the ground. They shimmered faintly along the snow, winding through forests, fields and city streets.

No one knew their source. People followed them for fun, for superstition or for curiosity.

Jalen followed them for hope.

He had lost his job recently and felt unmoored. When he stepped outside late one evening and saw the shimmering trails stretching across the quiet street, he felt pulled toward them.

He followed one trail as it wound through a park. The silver light reflected softly on the snow. The trail led him to a bench where an older man sat feeding birds.

Jalen hesitated.

The man smiled. "You look like someone searching for something."

"Maybe," Jalen replied. "Or maybe I am simply lost."

The man patted the bench. Jalen sat.

They spoke for a long while. The man shared stories of years lived, paths taken, mistakes made, and joys found. Jalen felt lighter as he listened. When he finally stood, the trail had grown brighter beneath his feet.

"Follow it until you reach the end," the man said. "It always leads where you need to go."

Jalen walked until the silver trail stopped at the steps of the community center. A sign in the window read, Volunteers needed for winter programs.

A sense of direction stirred inside him. He stepped inside and was greeted with warm smiles.

The silver trails vanished by morning, but Jalen's new purpose remained.

The Hearthkeeper

In the village, there were stories of a figure called the Hearthkeeper. A winter spirit, some said. A wandering guardian, others claimed. People believed the Hearthkeeper visited homes that burned with kindness, adding warmth to their fires during the coldest nights.

Most dismissed the tale as folklore. Yet one winter evening, a faint knock sounded on Rowan's door. She lived alone in a small cottage with a stone hearth and a handmade quilt draped over her chair.

When she opened the door, no one stood outside. Only snow drifted gently on the porch. But a small bundle wrapped in cloth lay at her feet.

Inside the cloth was a single log carved with swirling patterns. It smelled faintly of pine and spice.

Rowan set it in the fireplace. The moment it caught flame, the room filled with gentle warmth unlike any fire she had known. The flames glowed in hues of soft gold and pale blue.

She felt comfort settle into her bones. For the first winter in many years, loneliness loosened its grip.

The next morning, a set of footprints circled her cottage. Not human. Not animal. Something in between. Rowan touched the prints and whispered a quiet thank you.

She placed a candle in her window each evening afterward as a sign of gratitude.

Other villagers began finding similar carved logs during the season. Some by their doors. Some near their barns. Each log brought warmth that lasted longer than ordinary fire. People gathered together more often, sharing meals and stories, drawn by the gentle heat.

By spring, the logs vanished as mysteriously as they had arrived. Yet the village felt different. Closer. Kinder.

Rowan kept one small piece of the carved wood on her mantel. Its patterns reminded her that winter holds its own protectors.

And she believed the Hearthkeeper would return when needed.

Chapter 3
SERENDIPITY

Not every accident is random.
Some are soft arrangements,
where the world leans in
and whispers, "This way."

The Bus That Did Not Arrive

The 7:45 bus always arrived on time. It was so
reliable that people planned their mornings around
the sound of its brakes. One wet Thursday, however, it
did not come.

Rhea checked her watch, then the timetable, then her
watch again. Around her, others muttered and sighed.
A man in a navy coat paced. A teenager checked a
weather app. A woman with a red scarf hugged a
laptop bag to her chest.

At 7:52 the screen above the stop finally flickered. Service disruption. Next bus: 18 minutes.

A collective groan rose. Several people peeled away to call taxis. Rhea considered doing the same. She was already tired, already late in her mind. Rain tapped the shelter roof in soft, steady rhythms.

The woman in the red scarf caught her eye and gave a small, sympathetic smile.

"Guess we live here now," she joked.

Rhea laughed. "I will send for my mail."

The joke opened a door. They began to talk. About the weather first, then work, then how both of them had once dreamed of doing something completely different.

"I wanted to be an illustrator," the woman said. "But I blinked and somehow I became an office person with a drawer full of highlighters."

Rhea nodded. "I studied architecture. Now I mostly arrange furniture in other people's houses."

"Is that at least satisfying?" the woman asked.

"Sometimes. I like seeing spaces change. But I miss designing from the ground up."

The woman's eyes brightened. "I work at a small community arts center. We are starting a project to redesign our children's reading room. We cannot pay much, but we need someone with real design sense.

The last attempt made everything look like a waiting room for confused giraffes."

Rhea laughed. "That sounds impressive in a worrying way."

The woman grinned. "Come by, if you like. I am Noor." She pulled a flyer from her bag and scribbled a note with an email address.

The delayed bus finally pulled into the stop, headlights cutting through the rain. People crowded on with weary resignation.

Rhea found a seat by the window, Noor standing beside her in the aisle. They exchanged a final smile as the bus lurched forward.

All day, Rhea kept feeling the folded flyer in her pocket. That evening, instead of collapsing in front of the television, she opened her laptop and sent a short email.

Hello Noor. This morning's bus delay might have been a small gift. I would love to hear more about the reading room.

Weeks later, as she stood in a bright space filled with sketches, color swatches and the laughter of children trying out new beanbags, Rhea thought back to the morning when the bus did not come.

Sometimes lateness is not a loss. Sometimes it is a quiet invitation to take a different route entirely.

The Book That Fell Open

Elliot never planned to visit the secondhand bookshop that afternoon. He was on his way home, distracted, walking faster than usual, when a sudden gust of wind drove him under the nearest awning. The little bell above the shop door jingled as he ducked inside.

The air smelled of paper and dust and something like cinnamon. Stacks of books towered on every surface. A cat slept in a box labeled Travel.

He wandered toward the philosophy shelf without much aim, fingers brushing worn spines. As he turned a corner, his shoulder bumped a stack and a single paperback toppled off the top.

It landed at his feet, open.

Elliot bent to pick it up. The book was an old collection of essays. His gaze fell on a sentence on the exposed page: You are not late for your life. You are arriving exactly when your courage is ready.

His chest tightened.

He had spent weeks telling himself he had missed his chance. A chance to move cities. A chance to change careers. A chance to step away from a job that drained him.

He read the sentence again.

"Funny how books choose people," a voice said.

The shopkeeper, an older woman with silver hair wrapped in a loose bun, watched him from behind the counter.

"I knocked it over," Elliot said.

She smiled. "Accidents are sometimes only introductions."

He bought the book without really knowing why. On the train home he read the essay from the beginning. The writer described quitting a safe job at forty, moving to a new place, starting again. Not recklessly. Just honestly.

The words felt uncomfortably close to the thoughts he had been trying to ignore.

That evening, Elliot pulled out a notebook and wrote a list of the things he was afraid of losing if he left his job. Then a second list of what he was afraid of losing if he stayed. One list was longer. The decision did not become easy, but it became clearer.

Months later, after he had finally handed in his notice and was packing boxes for his move, the book fell from a shelf again, landing open on the same page.

He laughed softly, almost in disbelief.

"Thank you," he said, to no one in particular.

Some encounters are planned. Others arrive on a gust of wind, dressed as clumsy mistakes.

Two Seats on the Evening Train

The evening commuter train was crowded, as usual. Hana squeezed aboard and scanned for an empty seat. Only one remained, beside a man reading a thick technical manual.

She sat, tucking her bag between her feet, and tried to balance her sketchbook on her knees. The train jolted forward. Her pencil slid, scratching a dark line across the half finished drawing of a city street.

She sighed.

"Bad timing?" the man asked without looking up.

"You could say that," she replied. "I was trying to give this building a nice clean edge. Now it looks like it survived an earthquake."

He glanced at the sketch. "I like it. The imperfection gives it character."

Hana studied the ruined line. It did look oddly dynamic, as if the building were stretching.

"You really think so?" she asked.

He nodded. "I design structures for a living. Things that bend are often stronger than things that break."

She smiled. "You are an engineer?"

"Structural," he said. "You are an artist?"

"Trying to be. I draw cities I have not visited yet."

He pointed to the page. "What city is this one?"

"Somewhere I might move to," she admitted. "If I gather enough courage."

He tapped the margin near the crooked line. "Then perhaps this is not a mistake. Maybe it is a sign that your cities do not need to be perfect before you step into them."

They fell into easy conversation. He told her about bridges and load bearing walls. She told him about colors and skylines. The train nearly missed its stops as they spoke.

At her station, Hana closed the sketchbook. "Thank you for rescuing my drawing from the recycling bin."

"Thank you for reminding me that buildings can be art," he replied.

As she rose to leave, he reached into his pocket and handed her a small business card. On the back he had written: When you are ready to draw a real city, call me. I can tell you which bridges are worth sketching.

She laughed and slipped the card into her sketchbook.

Months later, when she finally did move to the city she had been drawing, that card guided one of her first walks. They met again on a real bridge this time, with the river moving steadily beneath them.

Looking back, she realized that if any other seat had been free that evening, her life might have unfolded along a very different line.

The Misprinted Invitation

The invitation was meant for apartment 3B, not 3A. The courier slipped the envelope under the wrong door and continued through the building.

Jon, who lived in 3A, almost tossed it out. He had no upcoming events and assumed it was junk. Yet the paper felt too thick, the handwriting too careful. He opened it.

Inside was a simple card:

You are warmly invited to a small gathering of neighbors, to celebrate stories, tea and winter light. Saturday, 7 p.m. Rooftop.

He had lived in the building for two years and could not recall speaking to anyone beyond a brief hello in the stairwell. He nearly put the invitation aside, then paused.

Stories, tea and winter light sounded exactly like the kind of evening he wished he knew how to find.

On Saturday, curiosity won. He climbed the stairs to the rooftop, rehearsing a polite apology for the misunderstanding.

The rooftop had been transformed. String lights hung in loose arcs. Folding chairs circled low tables. A thermos of hot chocolate steamed beside plates of biscuits. A woman stood near the entrance, adjusting a tray.

She turned as Jon stepped into the light. "You must be from 3B," she said.

"Actually, I am from 3A," he replied. "I think there was a delivery error. I can go if this is awkward. I only wanted to return the invitation."

For a second she looked startled. Then she laughed. "Maybe the error belongs to the courier. The invitation seems to have delivered you exactly where you needed to be."

She introduced herself as Lina. Slowly, other neighbors arrived, some shyer than others. A man from 4C brought a tin of homemade cookies. A couple from 2A carried a portable speaker that played soft jazz.

They took turns sharing short stories from their lives. Small ones. Funny ones. Quiet ones. Jon listened, surprised by how fond he felt toward people he had previously passed without noticing.

When it was his turn, he admitted how the invitation had found him by mistake.

Lina smiled. "I like that even more. Serendipity is the best event planner."

At the end of the night, as people folded chairs and blew out candles, Lina handed Jon a second card. This one was handwritten on plain paper.

Next time you will not need an excuse to join us.

He pinned it to his fridge.

Weeks later, he still smiled each time he opened the door and saw it. Friendship had arrived because a courier misread a letter. Life, he decided, had a sense of humor.

The Rainstorm Detour

On the day of the unexpected storm, Callum forgot his umbrella at home. The morning had been clear. By lunchtime, the sky had darkened into a heavy quilt.

He left work hoping to outrun the rain, but the first drops hit his shoulders halfway down the street. Within seconds, the downpour became complete. People scattered for cover.

Callum ducked into the nearest doorway, which belonged to a small shop he had never noticed. A bell chimed as he stepped inside.

The place was filled with plants. Hanging vines, pots of herbs, small trees stretching toward the ceiling. The air smelled of soil and citrus.

"Welcome," a voice said from behind a row of ferns.

A woman emerged, wiping her hands on a cloth. "I see the storm has delivered another traveler."

Callum laughed. "I just needed somewhere dry."

"Well, you found somewhere green too."

He wandered between the plants, reading little signs. Hopeful Basil. Patient Rosemary. Optimistic Fern. Each pot had a small tag with a personality trait.

"Do you name them yourself?" he asked.

"I do," she replied. "People seem more willing to care for a plant that has a story."

He paused at a small fig tree with a sign that read, Learns Late but Learns Well.

"This one feels familiar," he said.

She smiled. "I like that one. It had a difficult start but refuses to give up."

The rain intensified outside, drumming against the windows. Inside, the shop glowed warm. They spoke about small beginnings and second chances. Callum admitted he felt stuck in a job that paid his bills but did not nourish him.

The woman nodded. "This shop used to be my father's hardware store. Everyone expected me to keep selling nails and screws. Instead, I turned it into a greenhouse. People thought I was foolish. But sometimes you have to grow your own weather."

Callum absorbed the phrase. Grow your own weather.

When the rain finally eased, he stood near the door, reluctant to leave the green calm.

"Take the fig," she said.

"I cannot," he protested.

"You can," she insisted. "It wants a place where someone understands that learning late is still learning."

He walked home cradling the small tree, the air fresh and cool. The storm had scrubbed the sky clear.

Months later, the fig tree thrived on his windowsill. Each time he watered it, he remembered the plant shop and the woman who turned hardware into leaves. The idea of growing his own weather stayed with him until he finally began applying for different work.

It still rained sometimes. Life did not stop throwing storms. But he no longer saw them only as inconvenience. Some were simply detours into new rooms he might otherwise never have entered.

The Wrong Number Message

The text arrived just after midnight.

Thank you for today. I did not know I needed that walk until we were halfway through it. Sleep well.

Leah blinked at her phone. She had spent the evening alone. No walk. No company. Clearly, someone had typed the wrong number.

Her first impulse was to ignore it. Then she thought of the sender, believing they had reached a friend. She replied.

I think you have the wrong person, but your message made me smile. I am glad you had a good day.

A few minutes later, the phone buzzed again.

Oh no, I am so sorry. That is embarrassing. Wrong number indeed. I hope your day was at least tolerable.

Leah stared at the screen. It had been more than tolerable, but also more lonely than she liked to admit.

It was quiet, she wrote. But your message improved it.

There was a pause, then another text.

In that case, I am glad my mistake landed somewhere it could help. I will let you sleep. Sweet dreams, mystery stranger.

Over the next week, the wrong number became less of a mistake and more of a thread. Short exchanges appeared at odd times.

A photo of a beautiful sunset with the caption, Look at this sky.

A message saying, I passed an exam I was nervous about.

A simple, How is your corner of the world today?

Leah replied with small pieces of her life. A picture of her overwatered succulent. A confession about trying a new recipe and burning half of it. A comment about the kindness of the librarian who always saved her favorite books.

Neither shared names. It felt like a small secret corridor in the day.

One evening, after a particularly rough day at work, Leah sent a longer message.

Today was heavy. I felt invisible most of the time. If you have any spare encouragement, I will gladly borrow some.

The reply came quickly.

You are not invisible. You are someone whose words have brightened a stranger's week. That alone means you matter more than you know.

She felt tears prick her eyes.

Weeks later, they finally exchanged first names. He was Jonah. She was Leah. They still kept details light, but the connection felt real.

Eventually, they arranged a cautious meeting at a public cafe. Two people who might never have crossed paths if a single digit in a phone number had not gone astray.

When they recognized each other from shared photos of mugs and notebooks, they laughed at the absurdity and the rightness of it.

Some errors are not errors at all. They are doors in disguise.

The Coat with Two Histories

Mara found the coat in a thrift shop on a quiet side street. It was a deep green wool, lined with soft fabric, just her size. The price tag surprised her. Far too low for such good material.

She tried it on. It fit as if made for her, the sleeves just right, the collar falling neatly around her neck.

Inside the left pocket she felt something folded. Later, at home, she reached in and pulled out a small photograph. It showed a couple standing on a snowy bridge, laughing mid movement. On the back someone had written, First winter together.

Mara smiled. The coat had belonged to someone with a story. She wondered whether they had outgrown it or moved away or simply forgotten the photograph in its pocket.

She wore the coat often. It kept her warm on long walks through the park. Each time she slipped it on, she felt accompanied.

One evening, while sitting on a bench, a woman approached slowly.

"I am sorry to bother you," the woman said. "But I think that coat used to be mine."

Mara stood, startled. "I bought it from the shop on Evergreen."

The woman nodded. "I donated it last year. I thought it had served its time. Seeing it again feels like bumping into an old friend."

Mara hesitated, then asked, "Were you on a bridge in winter, perhaps?"

The woman's eyes widened. "You found the photograph."

Mara handed it to her. "It was in the pocket."

The woman held the picture gently. "We took this on the day we decided to move here. We were freezing, but we wanted proof that we were brave enough to start over."

Mara gestured to the bench. They sat. The woman, whose name was Lila, told her about the move, the relationship that had since ended, and the decision to donate the coat when she felt ready to shed that chapter.

"I am glad it found someone kind," Lila said softly.

"It has carried me through my own transitions," Mara

replied. "I left a job I hated this year. This coat has seen more walks of uncertainty than I can count."

Lila smiled. "Then it is doing exactly what it should."

Before they parted, Lila wrote her number on the back of the photograph and gave it back to Mara.

"Keep it," she said. "Let it remind you that clothes, like people, can have more than one good story."

Mara slipped the photograph back into the pocket, feeling that the coat now carried two histories instead of one.

Sometimes you inherit more than fabric when you choose something secondhand. Sometimes you inherit courage.

The Coffee Receipt

The cafe printed little quotes at the bottom of its receipts. Most people ignored them. They were usually generic lines about kindness or patience.

One morning, Alex ordered his usual black coffee. The barista handed him the cup and receipt with a practiced smile. He stuffed the receipt into his pocket without glancing at it.

Later, at his desk, he reached for a pen and the receipt slipped out. He almost threw it away, then saw the line printed at the bottom.

You will meet someone today who helps you remember who you used to be.

He chuckled. "Predictive receipts now," he muttered.

At lunch, he wandered into the small park behind his office. A woman sat on a bench sketching the fountain. He would have walked past, but something about her posture felt familiar.

She looked up, surprised. "Alex?"

It was Hana, an old friend from university. They had not seen each other in nearly ten years.

They stared for a moment, then laughed, both a little shocked by the sudden collision of past and present.

They spent the hour catching up. She showed him the sketch, all quick lines and soft shading, identical in style to the drawings she used to pin on dorm walls. He remembered how she used to pull him away from endless study sessions to wander the city.

"You taught me how to notice things," he said. "I have not done enough of that lately."

She tilted her head. "I remember you as the one who always had ideas for stories. Do you still write?"

He hesitated. "Not really. Spreadsheets have replaced stories."

"That seems like a poor trade," she replied gently.

When lunch ended, they exchanged numbers. As he walked back to the office, he pulled the receipt from his pocket again.

You will meet someone today who helps you remember who you used to be.

He shook his head, smiling. The quote was generic, yes, but its timing wrapped it in a new kind of meaning.

That night, instead of opening his laptop for more work, Alex opened an old file of unfinished writing. The words felt stiff at first, then slowly began to move.

The receipt ended up taped to the corner of his desk.

Sometimes the world nudges you through tiny printed letters that most people never see.

The Library Chair

The fourth floor of the central library was almost always quiet. It housed old periodicals, bound dissertations and a single orange armchair that looked wildly out of place among the muted shelves.

Naomi chose that chair because it stood near a large window. She visited on Sundays to read in the light that pooled around it.

One afternoon, she arrived to find someone already sitting there. A man with dark curly hair, absorbed in a thick novel. He noticed her hovering.

"Sorry," he said, half rising. "Do you usually sit here?"

She flushed. "No, please stay. There are other seats."

He stepped aside. "We can share it. It is bigger than it looks."

They arranged themselves carefully, sitting at opposite edges with books balanced on their knees. It should have felt awkward, but the absurdity softened the edges of their shyness.

"What brings you to the forgotten floor?" he asked.

"Silence," she replied. "And this chair."

"Same," he said. "I like the way the light lands here. Makes even difficult books feel kinder."

They read for a while, side by side, turning pages at different speeds. Occasionally one of them would smile at something, and the other would ask, "Good part?" without looking up.

When the sun shifted and shadows lengthened, they closed their books.

"I am Naomi," she said.

"Lucas," he replied.

The next Sunday, Naomi arrived earlier. The chair was empty. She settled in with her book, feeling oddly disappointed.

Five minutes later, Lucas appeared, slightly out of breath.

"I was hoping you would be here," he said.

They shared the chair again.

This became their quiet routine. Sundays in the orange chair, reading, exchanging brief comments, occasionally recommending books to each other. Neither pushed for more. The simple companionship felt enough.

One weekend, Naomi's day went badly. The bus was late, her bag strap broke and her coffee spilled down her sleeve. She nearly went straight home, but the thought of the chair pulled her to the library.

Lucas was already there, holding two cups.

"I guessed your coffee order," he said. "It seemed like a tea day."

She laughed, tension dissolving. "You guessed correctly."

They sat, and the chair felt warmer than usual.

Years later, when the library renovated the fourth floor, the orange chair was scheduled to be removed. Naomi and Lucas, now firmly woven into each other's lives, visited on the final day of the old layout.

The librarian smiled at them. "You two should know, that chair is being donated to the small reading room down the street. It seems to have a talent for bringing people together."

Naomi and Lucas exchanged a look. Serendipity, it seemed, favored comfortable seating.

The Coin at the Crosswalk

The old coin lay near the crosswalk button, half buried in slush. Most people stepped over it. Tom did too at first, then doubled back. Something about the dull glint caught his eye.

He picked it up and rubbed it with his thumb. It was heavier than a modern coin, stamped with an unfamiliar crest and a year so worn it was almost unreadable.

Curiosity stirred. He slipped it into his pocket and crossed the street.

At lunch, he showed it to the waitress at the small diner he frequented.

"That looks antique," she said, squinting. "You should show it to my grandfather. He collects coins. He is in the back room most days pretending to work."

She returned a few minutes later with an elderly man who introduced himself as Samir. His hands trembled slightly as he examined the coin.

"This is from my home country," he said softly. "I have not seen one in decades."

Tom leaned forward. "Is it valuable?"

"In money, no," Samir replied. "In memory, yes."

He told a story about buying sweet bread with coins like that as a boy, about a market that smelled of spices and oranges, about pockets jangling with possibility.

Tom listened, captivated. The coin had transported the man across years and oceans.

"I did not expect a simple walk to do this," Samir said, smiling.

Tom felt a sudden urge. "You should keep it," he said. "It means more to you."

Samir shook his head. "You found it. Perhaps it is meant to remind you that small things can open large doors."

The waitress arrived with Tom's usual sandwich. "Granddad will talk all day if you let him," she said fondly.

Tom grinned. "I do not mind. I like doors."

Over the next weeks, Tom visited the diner more often. He brought other small curiosities he found on his walks. Buttons, a feather, an old key. Each sparked a story from Samir.

Their conversations grew. Through them, Tom realized how much of his own life he had been walking through on autopilot.

One day, as he waited at the same crosswalk, he felt the coin in his pocket and decided to take a different street home. That small choice led him past a community notice board advertising a volunteer position at a local museum.

He applied. He was accepted.

Months later, he and Samir visited the museum together. They stood in front of a glass case filled with old coins. Tom held his own in his fist, feeling its warmth.

Some objects, he thought, are not just relics. They are quiet messengers.

And sometimes, the message is simply this: pay attention. The world is full of crossings that lead somewhere new.

The Flower Left on the Bench

Every morning, Aria stopped at the small park bench near her office. She rarely sat, but she liked the way sunlight pooled around the little clearing. One crisp spring morning, a single daisy lay on the bench, fresh and bright.

She looked around. No one seemed to be paying attention. She left the flower where it was and hurried to work.

The next day, another daisy appeared. And the day after that. Sometimes a single bloom. Sometimes two. Always on the same bench. Always fresh.

Aria began to look forward to the small surprise. It felt like a gentle greeting from the world.

One morning she arrived earlier than usual and spotted a young man placing a daisy carefully on the bench. He stepped back, adjusting the stem so it faced the path.

Aria approached. "Are these yours?"

He startled, then smiled. "Yes. I leave them for anyone who might need a small bit of luck."

"That is wonderfully strange," she said.

"I prefer quietly hopeful," he replied. "I started last year when I was recovering from a rough season. Leaving small good things made the days feel lighter."

They talked briefly. His name was Julian. He worked nights at the bakery across the street and often ended his shift with this ritual.

Aria reached to touch the daisy. "It always makes my morning brighter."

Julian's expression softened. "Then I am glad. I hoped someone felt that."

After that morning, Aria sometimes brought her own flower. A tulip. A sprig of lavender. A marigold from her balcony garden. Occasionally Julian arrived at the same time and they exchanged smiles or short conversations, never long enough to intrude on the quiet magic of the ritual.

One day the bench held no flower at all. Aria waited a few moments, puzzled. Then Julian rushed into the park carrying a small pot of blooming daisies.

"I thought we should plant something that stays," he said breathlessly.

They placed the pot beside the bench. The flowers lifted their bright heads toward the sun.

Aria and Julian sat for a moment, enjoying the gentle stillness.

Some rituals begin by accident. Others by intention. This one grew from a daisy on a bench and unfolded into something warm enough to stay.

The Painting That Was Not for Sale

The art market bustled each Saturday with vendors selling canvases, ceramics and handmade jewelry. Maya wandered the aisles often, searching for something she could not name.

One morning, a small painting caught her eye. It hung near the back of a tent, half hidden behind larger works. The painting showed a quiet street at dusk with soft lights in the windows and a cat crossing the road. The colors glowed with gentle melancholy.

Maya approached the vendor. "How much is this one?"

The vendor hesitated. "That painting is not for sale."

She blinked. "Oh. I am sorry. I did not mean to overstep."

"No, it is nothing like that," the vendor said gently. "My late brother painted it. I bring it with me because it helps me feel like he is here. But people ask about it often."

Maya touched her heart instinctively. "It is beautiful. It feels like home somehow."

The vendor looked thoughtful. "Would you tell me why?"

Maya explained that she had grown up in a small town that looked almost exactly like the street in the painting. She had been feeling unsettled since moving away. The painting reminded her of evenings when life felt slower and easier.

The vendor listened quietly. "You sound like someone who misses a place that no longer exists exactly as you remember it."

"That is exactly it."

The vendor smiled softly. "He used to paint places that felt like memories. I think he would be glad someone connected with it."

Maya stepped back. "I would never ask you to part with it."

The vendor nodded. "I know. But sometimes paintings find the person who needs them next."

The vendor wrapped the canvas carefully and handed it to her.

Maya protested, but the vendor simply said, "Consider it a gift from one person who misses a quiet street to another."

At home, Maya hung the painting above her desk. It changed the atmosphere of the room. Softer. Warmer. She found herself writing letters again, cooking recipes from her childhood, calling her mother more often.

A month later, she returned to the market with a small framed photograph of her hometown at dusk. She handed it to the vendor. "I thought you might like to know where your brother's painting led me."

The vendor placed the photograph beside her booth, smiling. "It seems he is still connecting people."

Some art asks to be bought. Some asks to be admired. And some chooses its own way home.

The Coincidence Café

The café on Lark Street was ordinary except for one thing. Every table had a bowl filled with scraps of paper on which patrons wrote tiny coincidences that had happened to them. Some were funny. Some were touching. Some were so strange that people wondered if they could possibly be true.

Theo discovered the place on a rainy afternoon when he ducked inside for shelter. As he waited for his drink, he read the notes in a nearby bowl.

Found my lost earring after dreaming of it.

Ran into my childhood neighbor in a city of two million.

Said I wanted a dog. Adopted one the next day by accident.

Theo laughed softly.

The barista, a cheerful woman with short curls, said, "People like to notice little miracles. It keeps the world interesting."

Theo nodded. "I like the idea."

"Then write one," she said, sliding a blank slip toward him.

Theo thought. He wrote: Spilled coffee on my shirt today which forced me to change clothes and leave the house later than planned. Ran into an old friend I had not seen in years. Best delayed morning I ever had.

He dropped the note into the bowl and found a table.

As he drank his coffee, a woman approached holding his note.

"Did you write this?" she asked.

He felt embarrassed. "Yes. Sorry if that was arrogant to share."

She shook her head. "Not arrogant. Familiar."

She explained that she too had run into an old friend unexpectedly the previous week after missing a bus. They compared stories and laughed. The conversation flowed effortlessly.

Her name was Serena. She worked at a community theater. She invited Theo to attend an improv night. He agreed before he had time to talk himself out of it.

They met again the following week, then again. The café became their regular spot. Each visit, they wrote new notes about their small coincidences.

One afternoon, Theo reached into the bowl and found a slip he did not remember writing.

It read: I met someone here by accident. I think it might matter.

He looked up. Serena sat across from him, smiling.

"Yours?" he asked.

"Maybe," she said.

They held the moment gently, knowing that

coincidence had shaped something more than a story for the bowl.

Some cafés serve pastries and coffee. Others serve reminders that chance has a kind touch.

The Umbrella Swap

During an unexpected drizzle, Soren rushed into a convenience store to buy an umbrella. Only one remained, bright yellow with tiny raindrop patterns.

He paid and hurried to his appointment. By the time he arrived, the rain had stopped. He placed the umbrella in the stand near the door and forgot about it.

When he left an hour later, he grabbed the only yellow umbrella in the stand. He walked halfway down the block before noticing the handle was carved with initials.

This was not his umbrella.

He hurried back, but the stand now held a different umbrella. A navy one with a small note taped to it.

Accidental trade. Please enjoy this umbrella for now. It kept me dry for years. Consider it on loan.

Signed, S.

Soren chuckled. A borrowed umbrella from a stranger. He kept it, intending to return it if he ever found the owner.

The navy umbrella was sturdy and elegant. People often complimented it. Soren felt oddly proud of a thing that was not his.

One windy morning, the umbrella flipped inside out, and a passing woman caught it before it blew away.

"Careful," she said, laughing. "This weather is dramatic today."

Soren thanked her, then noticed her initials on a silver charm attached to her bag.

"Are you S?" he asked.

She blinked. "Do you mean the umbrella note?"

He held up the navy umbrella.

She gasped. "You found it. Or I suppose I found you."

They exchanged stories. She had taken his yellow umbrella by mistake, realized it too late and left the navy one as a fair trade until they could cross paths.

"Serendipity has good timing," she said.

They agreed to meet for tea to properly swap back. They did, though neither wanted to give up their borrowed umbrellas. They eventually solved it by exchanging them permanently.

Some items find their way to the right hands through curious detours. Some people do too.

The Unsent Email

Marcel drafted an email late one night after a draining workday. He meant to send it to his colleague, apologizing for a miscommunication during a project. He wanted to clear the air before the next morning.

The email was honest, perhaps too honest. After writing it, he hesitated, then closed his laptop without pressing send.

The next day, he arrived at work braced for tension. Instead, his colleague greeted him warmly.

"I thought about yesterday," she said. "You were under pressure. I was too. Let us reset."

Marcel breathed easier. Maybe the unsent email was unnecessary after all.

At lunch he opened his laptop and saw the draft still waiting. Something nudged him to read it again. His words felt vulnerable but sincere. He wondered why it felt easier to be generous on a screen than face to face.

He deleted it.

As he closed the tab, another draft appeared. One he did not remember writing.

It was a message he had once started to send to an old friend with whom he had lost contact. They had parted after a misunderstanding that neither had properly addressed.

Marcel had written the first lines but abandoned them years earlier. Seeing the unfinished draft now made his heart thud.

He reread the few sentences. They carried old emotion but also a softness he had forgotten he was capable of.

Something in him shifted.

That evening, he wrote a new message. Not long. Not heavy. Just a gentle reaching out.

I hope you have been well. I found an old draft today that reminded me of better days. If you ever feel like reconnecting, I would like that.

He pressed send before he could talk himself out of it.

An hour later, a reply arrived.

I have missed you. I thought it was too late to say so. Thank you for opening the door.

Marcel closed his eyes and let out a breath he had held for far too long.

Some messages do not need to be sent. Others wait years for the moment courage arrives.

The Map With No Streets

Jia loved old maps. She collected them from thrift stores, flea markets and estate sales. One afternoon her favorite shopkeeper handed her a curious sheet of parchment.

"No streets," he said, smiling. "Just shapes."

Indeed, the map showed a scattering of dots and lines with no labels. A few curves hinted at rivers, but nothing else resembled a real place.

"I cannot catalog it," he said. "Maybe you can enjoy it purely as mystery."

Jia bought the map and hung it above her desk. Over the next weeks she found herself drawn to its strange emptiness. Some days it looked like a constellation. Other days like a diagram of paths yet to be taken.

One evening, as she returned home, she noticed a man standing outside her building holding an identical map.

He looked up, startled. "Sorry. I was told someone here bought the companion map."

Jia blinked. "Companion?"

He held his map beside hers. When placed together, the dots aligned and the lines formed a complete pattern. Still not a recognizable city, but now a whole design.

"It is part of an art project," he explained. "My friend scattered twenty pairs of these maps across the city to see who would connect."

Jia smiled. "She succeeded."

They spent an hour discussing what the completed pattern resembled. A branching river system. A dance diagram. A story told sideways.

The man, Jonah, was an illustrator. He enjoyed creating images that encouraged people to find hidden meanings. They discovered they shared a love for visual puzzles, wandering neighborhoods and quiet cafés.

They agreed to meet the next weekend to walk the city and look for shapes that matched the map.

They never found a perfect match. That was not really the point. The map had already achieved its purpose.

Some paths are not meant to guide you somewhere specific. They simply introduce you to someone walking a similar way.

The Sandwich Mix-up

Every weekday morning, Callie bought the same sandwich from the deli near her office. Egg, arugula and pesto. She loved its simplicity.

One morning she arrived at her desk, unwrapped the paper and discovered a completely different sandwich. Roasted peppers, goat cheese and something sweet she could not identify.

She sighed. But since she was too hungry to return to the deli, she took a bite.

It was delicious.

She called the deli to inform them, more amused than upset. The manager apologized and explained another customer must have received hers by mistake.

Half an hour later, her phone buzzed with a text from an unknown number.

Hi. I think I ate your sandwich. If yours tastes like roasted peppers and joy, I am sorry.

Callie laughed. So I guess I ate yours. And it was excellent.

She received a reply. Shall we call this breakfast diplomacy? I propose a treaty. Tomorrow we meet at the deli and trade properly.

The next morning, she arrived early and found a man standing outside holding two sandwiches. He had kind eyes and a slightly embarrassed smile.

"I am Ben," he said. "Sandwich thief by accident."

"I am Callie," she replied. "Victim of misplaced pesto."

They traded sandwiches but decided to split them instead. They sat on a nearby bench and talked until the workday called them back.

The sandwich mix-up became a running joke. Sometimes they deliberately ordered wrong sandwiches to taste new combinations. Sometimes they simply met because mornings felt brighter that way.

One day, Ben admitted, "I am glad they miswrapped the orders that morning."

Callie nodded. "Me too. Breakfast diplomacy works better than most strategies."

Some connections begin with grand gestures. Others begin with a mislabeled sandwich wrapped in deli paper.

The Last Seat at the Lecture

The auditorium was full when Amina arrived. She had rushed across campus for a guest lecture on creativity in design, a topic she loved. Only one seat remained, tucked between a stack of backpacks and a young man scribbling furiously in a notebook.

"Is this taken?" she asked.

He looked up, startled. "No, please. Sit. Sorry for the chaos. I write messily when excited."

She smiled and slid into the seat.

The lecture began. The speaker talked about playful thinking, accidents that lead to breakthroughs and the importance of observing small details. Amina nodded eagerly. The young man beside her scribbled even faster.

Halfway through the talk, the speaker asked the audience to turn to a stranger and share one creative idea they had abandoned too soon.

Amina glanced at her neighbor.

He laughed nervously. "Well. I guess that is us."

They shared their abandoned ideas. She described a project involving recycled materials for public art installations. He described a storytelling platform built from community interviews.

"You should finish yours," he urged.

"You should finish yours," she replied.

After the lecture, they continued talking as they walked down the steps. His name was Daniel. They exchanged thoughts about creative blocks, the terror of starting again and the strange joy of chasing ideas that might fail.

At the exit, Daniel hesitated. "Would you like to exchange contact info? Maybe hold each other accountable to actually finish something."

Amina hesitated only a moment. "Yes. I would."

Over the next months, they met regularly to brainstorm, encourage each other and push through stalled moments. They collaborated on a small project for a campus festival. Their creative partnership sharpened both of them.

One evening, Amina admitted, "If that last seat had been taken, I would have gone home."

Daniel smiled. "Then I am very glad the universe saved it for you."

Some opportunities arrive disguised as inconvenience. Some partnerships begin when only one seat remains.

The Errand Route

Sam took the same route every Saturday for errands. Grocery store, dry cleaner, bakery. Predictable, efficient, comfortable. One morning the bakery was unexpectedly closed for renovations, forcing him to take a detour down a street he rarely traveled.

As he passed a narrow alley, a chalkboard sign caught his eye.

Open Studio Today. Free to wander. Free to wonder.

Curiosity tugged. He stepped inside.

The space was filled with sculptures, paintings and small installations made from everyday objects. A woman sat on the floor assembling something from driftwood and wire.

She looked up. "Welcome. You are here for the wandering?"

"I suppose so," Sam said, uncertain but intrigued.

"Then wander," she replied cheerfully.

He moved slowly through the space. One sculpture was made of broken spoons arranged like feathers. Another was a tower of stacked notebooks that seemed to lean without falling.

Sam felt unexpectedly moved. The art looked like someone had taken ordinary moments and rearranged them into possibility.

The woman approached. "I am Talia. This place is my attempt at a living sketchbook."

"It is wonderful," Sam said. "Unexpected."

"That is the goal. I like catching people off guard with gentleness."

She handed him a small wooden token. "Take this. It is part of the studio. If you carry it, you agree to see your routine differently."

He laughed. "Is that a contract?"

"A soft one," she answered.

He slipped the token into his pocket.

Sam began visiting weekly. Some pieces changed. Some disappeared. Some appeared in new corners. Each time he felt something loosen inside him.

Eventually he volunteered to assist during weekend workshops, helping children build sculptures from found materials. The work felt nourishing in a way he had not realized he needed.

One day, as he helped sweep the floor, Talia said, "You walk differently now. Less hurried. More awake."

Sam smiled. "I think your detour captured me."

"Good," she replied. "The world has more corners than most people visit."

He never returned to his old route completely. Some places deserve a permanent addition to the map of a life.

The Lighthouse Signal

During coastal storms, the lighthouse near Rowan's cottage shone its beam in long, sweeping arcs. She often watched it through her window during sleepless nights. The light steadied her.

One stormy evening, as she walked the shoreline to clear her mind, she noticed the lighthouse beam flicker in a strange rhythm. It almost looked intentional, like a pattern.

She paused. The beam flashed twice, then again after a short interval.

Rowan frowned. She had always been good with patterns. This one tugged at her memory. It resembled an old code she had learned in a childhood club.

Two flashes meant someone nearby was signaling for notice.

Rowan hesitated only a moment before heading up the path to the lighthouse.

Inside, she found the keeper, an older man named Corin, sitting at a small desk. He looked up, surprised.

"You saw it," he said.

"I thought you might need help," Rowan said.

Corin smiled faintly. "Not help exactly. Company. The storm is heavy tonight, and the light often draws people inward, not outward. I wondered if anyone would notice."

They shared tea while wind rattled the windows. Rowan confessed she had been feeling isolated during the long winter. Corin admitted the storm season often left him lonelier than he liked to admit.

The beam continued its steady sweep across the waves.

"Do you ever feel," Rowan asked, "that the lighthouse

is not just guiding ships, but guiding people who are adrift in quieter ways?"

Corin nodded. "It has done that for me countless nights."

They spoke until the storm softened. Before she left, Corin handed her a small key.

"This opens the side door," he said. "If you ever see the beam flicker twice again, come up. It will mean the kettle is on."

Rowan laughed. "All right. And if I ever flash a lantern twice from the cliff, it will mean I could use a conversation."

He nodded solemnly. "Then I will expect you."

Through winter, they shared many evenings at the lighthouse. The light swept across the water, a calm reminder of connection formed through an unexpected signal.

Some beacons are built for ships. Others shine for people who still need a place to anchor.

Chapter 4

QUIET TRANSFORMATIONS

The Cup on the Windowsill

For years, Lena kept an old chipped mug on her kitchen windowsill. It had belonged to her former partner, who moved out one rainy afternoon and never came back for it. The mug held a small plant at first, then pens, then nothing but dust.

She told herself she left it there because she forgot it was not hers. Truthfully, it had become a monument to a life she had not fully accepted had ended.

One Sunday, as she washed dishes, she glanced at the mug and noticed a faint hairline crack running down its side. Sunlight caught the crack, turning it into a thin silver line.

She dried her hands and picked it up. It felt lighter than she remembered.

Without thinking too much, she carried it to the table and sat down. She traced the rim with her thumb. Good memories surfaced first, then difficult ones, then the long stretch of time afterward when she had tried not to feel anything at all.

The mug was only ceramic, she knew. But it held thirteen years of shared seasons in her mind. Leaving it on the sill had been easier than deciding what to do with the story it represented.

Lena stood and opened a cupboard. She brought out a small wooden box that usually held loose notes and receipts. She emptied it, then placed the mug carefully inside.

It did not feel like hiding. It felt like putting something tender into a quieter room.

Later that day she wiped the windowsill clean and set a new small plant there instead. A bright green trailing vine that a neighbor had given her. The sill looked oddly bare, then surprisingly fresh.

Over the next weeks, she noticed the difference. Mornings felt less like rewinding the same old film.

The empty space where the mug once sat became a place for new habits. Some days she rested her cup of tea there. Some days she placed a book. Some days she left it empty on purpose.

One evening, when a friend visited, they stood by the window and watched the sky deepen from blue to soft violet.

"It suits you," the friend said. "The space. The light."

Lena smiled. "It is small, but it feels like breathing room."

She did not mention the mug in the box. She did not need to. The change was not about erasing the past. It was about moving the weight of it from the center of her daily view to a shelf where it could rest.

Months later, when she stumbled across the box while tidying, she opened it without flinching. The mug was still chipped, still familiar, but it no longer held the same sharpness.

She closed the lid gently.

Quiet transformation, she realised, sometimes looks as simple as choosing what you see every day when you look out at the world.

The Message Left on Seen

Mara drafted the apology three times before she sent it. She and her brother had not spoken in almost a year, after an argument that grew larger than either of them intended. It started over an inheritance detail and spiraled into old grievances. Pride had done the rest.

Her message was short.

I miss you. I am sorry for my part in how things ended. If you ever feel like talking, I am here.

She pressed send and watched the status line change.

Delivered.

Seen.

Then nothing.

Minutes crawled forward, then hours. She tried not to check her phone, failed, checked again. No reply.

By evening, hurt crept in. Had she expected too much? Perhaps he was still angry. Perhaps he would never respond. The old ache of rejection opened again in her chest.

She set the phone on airplane mode and went to bed early.

The next morning, she woke with a different feeling. Disappointment still pulsed quietly, but underneath it was something steadier.

She had said what she needed to say. Kindly, clearly, without demand. It was not a magic spell. It was a door. Whether anyone walked through it was no longer something she could control.

For the first time in months, she felt a small shift inside. The weight of the argument no longer pressed quite as heavily on her shoulders. Responsibility had replaced helplessness.

Over the following days, she thought often about that quiet difference. When she picked up her phone, she no longer flinched. The message remained marked as seen. The lack of response hurt, but it did not define her reality.

She began making smaller changes with the same approach. Answering emails she had avoided. Admitting mistakes quickly at work instead of defending them. Saying thank you more often. Letting people know when she appreciated them.

Weeks later, her brother finally responded.

I needed time. I read your message and did not know how to answer. I am not ready for a long conversation, but I am willing to start with a short one.

They met for coffee at a quiet cafe. The talk was awkward at first, then steadier. Not everything was resolved. Not everything needed to be. They agreed to meet again.

That evening, Mara sat on her couch and thought about the hours when her message had sat on seen with no reply. She could have decided then that her effort had failed. Instead, something gentle had begun.

The transformation had not been in his response, though that mattered. It had started earlier, in her choice to speak honestly without controlling the outcome.

Quiet change sometimes begins in the space between sending and receiving, where we learn to live with unanswered echoes and still keep our hearts open.

The Shoes She Finally Replaced

The running shoes by the door were worn almost smooth. The soles had thinned, the fabric had frayed and one lace had been tied together in a permanent knot. Still, Nina kept them.

They were the shoes she wore during the hardest months of her life, when she ran not for fitness but to outrun a heartbreak that seemed to fill every room. Each step back then had felt like a plea.

Years passed. The pain softened into a quiet scar. She ran less often now, but the shoes remained by the door, as if ready to carry her through another emergency.

One afternoon, as she laced them up for a rare jog, the knot finally snapped. The lace came apart in her hands. She stared at it, surprised by the sting of tears.

She could have replaced the lace. She had spares in a drawer. Instead, she sat on the mat and held the shoe, suddenly aware of how long she had been clinging to it as proof of her endurance.

These shoes have done their job, she thought. Maybe it is time to let them rest.

The next day she visited a sports shop. The wall of bright new shoes felt overwhelming. A young clerk approached with an easy smile.

"Looking for anything in particular?" he asked.

"Something that feels like forward," she replied before she could phrase it more politely.

He considered this and nodded. "Then we will find a pair that feels light."

They tried several options. When she slipped into a pair of soft gray trainers with firm support, her feet felt strangely free. She jogged a short stretch down the store aisle. Each step landed differently, like a promise instead of a memory.

At home, she placed the old shoes in a paper bag. She did not throw them away that day. She left the bag in a corner and lived with the decision for a week.

In that time, she took several runs in the new shoes. The routes were similar, but the feeling was not. She no longer ran from anything. She ran to feel her lungs expand, to watch the sky change colors, to say hello to the quiet strength in her legs.

Finally, she carried the bag to a donation bin that accepted worn but usable gear for recycling. As she slid it inside, a wave of tenderness washed over her.

"Thank you," she whispered, to the shoes and to the version of herself who had needed them so desperately.

Walking home in her new trainers, she realised the change was not in the footwear. It was in the intention behind her steps.

Sometimes transformation sounds as simple as a different rhythm on the pavement.

The Plant She Almost Gave Up On

The spider plant in Leena's living room had spent months looking more like a collection of stubborn green threads than a thriving bit of life. Its leaves sagged. The soil stayed damp no matter how carefully she watered. She considered throwing it away more than once.

"I am clearly not meant to keep plants," she told a friend over video call, angling the camera toward the drooping leaves.

Her friend peered through the screen. "It looks thirsty for light, not water. Try moving it."

Leena glanced around the room. The plant had always sat on the low coffee table, far from the window. She had put it there years ago and never questioned the choice.

Later that day, she shifted it to the small balcony that caught the late afternoon sun. The air felt brighter there, cooler. She brushed dust from the leaves and gently loosened the top layer of soil.

The plant did not transform overnight. A week passed with little visible change. But Leena kept visiting it each evening. She checked the soil, rotated the pot and spoke to it softly even when she felt silly.

After two weeks, she noticed the first new shoot. A thin, pale green spear rising bravely from the base. She grinned.

"Look at you," she whispered. "You were not finished at all."

More shoots followed. The leaves lifted. The plant grew fuller. Tiny offshoots began to appear, reaching over the rim of the pot as if seeking more space.

Watching it recover shifted something in Leena's mind. She thought of areas in her own life she had written off as hopeless. Her half practiced guitar. Her abandoned language lessons. Friendships that had grown thin through neglect rather than harm.

Maybe, she thought, some parts of my life are not failing. They are just in the wrong corner.

She rearranged her days with the same gentle approach she had used with the plant. She moved her guitar to a visible spot. She scheduled a weekly language call with a friend abroad. She reached out with short messages to people she missed.

Nothing changed overnight. But gradually, she felt herself lean toward light she had been ignoring.

Months later, as she trimmed a healthy cascade of spider plant babies, she thought about how close she had come to throwing the whole thing away.

Some things do not need to be replaced. They only need to be moved where they can grow.

Quiet transformation often begins with the simple act of shifting something a few feet closer to the sun.

The Apology He Wrote for Himself

Oren kept replaying the same memory, a scene from five years earlier where he had lost his temper with a friend during a stressful project. He remembered every word he had said, every flinch on his friend's face, every moment of silence that followed. They had patched things up later, but the shame clung stubbornly inside him.

One cold evening, after yet another cycle of self-criticism, he sat at his desk and opened a blank document. He began to type.

Dear you, who spoke too sharply that day,

The letter flowed out faster than he expected. He described the pressure he had been under, the fear of failing, the exhaustion that sharpened his voice. He did not excuse his behavior, but he finally gave it context.

He wrote the apology he had already given his friend, then wrote the apology he had never given himself.

You were wrong, he typed, but you were trying. You could have done better, and now you know how. You do not need to carry this moment like a stone forever.

When he finished, he read the letter twice, then printed it. He folded the paper carefully and placed it in an envelope.

He did not know what to do with it. He could not mail it. It had no address. It was meant for the version of him who had walked away from that argument with shoulders stiff and jaw clenched, convinced he was irreparably flawed.

Finally he walked outside to the small park near his apartment. Under a bare tree, he sat on a bench and took out the envelope.

"I forgive you," he said quietly, feeling foolish and relieved at once.

He did not rip the letter or bury it. He simply read it out loud to the empty air, then slipped it back into his coat pocket.

In the days that followed, the memory still surfaced from time to time, but the sharpness had dulled. When it appeared, it brought with it not only the echo of his anger but also the words he had written afterward.

He noticed a small shift in the way he spoke to himself. Less condemnation. More curiosity. When he made new mistakes, he paused, acknowledged them and asked what could be learned instead of spiraling into familiar self blame.

Months later, he found the envelope while cleaning. He opened it and skimmed the letter, surprised to find it both old and new, like a note from someone who knew him well and wanted him to be kind.

He placed it in a box of keepsakes, not as a reminder of his worst day, but as proof that he had chosen a different way to live with it.

Sometimes the transformation is not in changing the past, but in changing the voice that narrates it.

The Train Ride Without Headphones

Every evening, Eli boarded the train home with headphones firmly in place. He listened to podcasts, music or nothing at all, using the sound as a curtain between himself and the crowded carriage.

One Tuesday, his headphones died halfway through the journey. The audio cut off mid sentence. He tapped the controls, checked the battery, even restarted his phone. Nothing.

He considered scrolling in silence, but the sudden absence of sound revealed a different layer of the train.

He heard the soft rustle of newspapers, the faint buzz of someone's game, the murmur of a child asking questions, the low rumble of two strangers debating which bakery sold the best cinnamon rolls.

Eli removed the headphones completely and slipped them into his bag.

He watched faces instead of screens. A woman stared out at her reflection in the window, lost in thought. An elderly man adjusted his scarf with deliberate care. A teenager balanced a sketchbook on her knees, shading a drawing of the carriage itself.

The train stopped unexpectedly between stations. A voice announced a short delay. A collective groan started, then faded.

The child nearby asked, "Are we stuck?"

"For a little while," her father replied.

"Is that bad?"

"Not if we decide it is just a pause," he said. "Sometimes pausing is good."

Eli smiled despite himself.

He caught the eye of the teenager with the sketchbook and nodded toward her drawing. "It looks great," he said softly.

She blinked, then smiled. "Thank you. I always hope someone will see it before I erase it."

For the remainder of the ride, Eli stayed present. No curated soundscape. Only the unfiltered rhythm of shared space.

That night, he left the headphones in his bag. The next day, he did the same.

He did not give them up entirely, but he began choosing at least one commute a week to take without them. On those days, he noticed more. The evolving graffiti outside the tunnel. The regular passengers whose faces had become familiar strangers. The way the carriage mood shifted with the weather.

He found himself feeling less detached from the city and more a part of the living fabric of it.

The change was small. No one else knew he had made it. Yet inside, a quiet channel had opened.

Transformation, he realised, does not always mean doing something dramatic. Sometimes it is as simple as listening to the world again.

The Mirror on Moving Day

On the day Kara moved out of the apartment she had shared with two roommates for years, she left packing the bathroom for last. The mirror above the sink had watched her through countless mornings and late night reflections. It had seen her arrive hopeful, endure heartbreak, laugh at inside jokes and practice interviews.

As she wiped dust from the corners, she caught her reflection and paused.

The woman looking back at her did not match the one who had moved in. Her hair was different, yes, but the change went deeper. There was a steadiness in her eyes that had not been there before. The shape of her posture had shifted, as if she carried herself rather than her worries.

She had spent weeks fixating on what she was leaving. Shared dinners, familiar streets, her favorite coffee place around the corner. But at that moment, the mirror showed her something else.

"You survived more than you thought you could," she whispered to herself.

She tried on the words again, louder. "You survived more than you thought you could."

They did not feel like a congratulation. They felt like a simple fact.

She remembered the night she cried on the bathroom floor after losing a job. The morning she stared at the mirror before a difficult conversation with a friend. The time she had rehearsed a speech for a presentation that terrified her.

Each time, she had doubted herself. Each time, she had gone on anyway.

She touched the cool glass, as if thanking it for bearing witness.

Later, as movers carried boxes out, one of her roommates commented, "You seem strangely calm."

"I think I am ready," Kara replied.

The roommate smiled. "You look it. Different, somehow."

That evening, in her new apartment, the bathroom mirror was smaller and not yet familiar. Kara set down a box of toiletries and caught her reflection again. She repeated the sentence from that morning.

"You survived more than you thought you could."

This time, she added, "And you will do it again."

Over the next months, she hung new art, learned different streets, found a new coffee place. Not every day felt confident. Some nights doubt visited quietly. But she had a different anchor now, a sentence that reminded her that the person in the mirror was not the sum of her fears.

Transformation had not happened on moving day. It had unfolded over years. The mirror had simply given her a moment to see it clearly.

Sometimes the biggest change is finally recognising who you have already become.

The Shelf She Cleared

The top shelf of Mina's wardrobe held a row of items she rarely touched. Old notebooks from a degree she never used. Souvenirs from trips that had ended friendships. A pile of neatly folded sweaters she had once loved but no longer wore.

"I will sort it someday," she always said.

One rainy afternoon, the someday arrived without ceremony. She opened the wardrobe to look for a scarf and felt an unexpected surge of irritation at the clutter above.

On impulse, she dragged a chair over and climbed up. One by one, she lifted the objects down.

The notebooks were filled with notes from classes she had taken to please her parents. She flipped through them and realised she remembered almost none of the content. The souvenirs were pretty but heavy with a sense of obligation to the past. The sweaters were soft but held the scent of a time when she had often ignored her own comfort to fit into someone else's preference.

Mina sat on the floor surrounded by items that represented versions of herself she had quietly outgrown.

She did not throw everything away. Some notebooks contained drawings worth keeping. One souvenir still made her smile. A single sweater felt like a genuine reflection of her taste.

The rest went into bags. She decided to donate what could be used by others and recycle what could not.

When the shelf was finally cleared, she wiped it clean and stood back. The empty space felt strangely powerful.

For a few days, she left it bare on purpose. Each time she opened the wardrobe, the gap greeted her with a sense of possibility. Nothing demanded that she fill it immediately.

Eventually, she placed a small box there containing only items that connected to who she was now. A journal from a recent trip she had chosen entirely for herself. A small plant that tolerated low light. A photo of her laughing with friends who knew her well.

The act of clearing the shelf did not change her life overnight. But it shifted the way she thought about what she held onto.

She became more aware of habits and obligations that no longer truly belonged to her. She said yes more thoughtfully. She allowed herself to say no without lengthy excuses.

Months later, when a friend mentioned feeling stuck because of old commitments, Mina thought of the shelf.

"Sometimes you have to climb up and see what you are carrying out of habit," she said.

Quiet transformation often begins with physical space. A drawer. A shelf. A corner of a room that finally reflects the person who lives there now.

The Phone Turned Face Down

Rafi had a habit of checking his phone during every lull. In queues, in conversations, in the few seconds while a kettle boiled. The screen waited like a small doorway he could step through whenever reality felt uncomfortable.

One evening, while having dinner with his sister, she paused mid sentence as his phone lit up again.

"I can wait," she said, not unkindly.

He looked up and saw the tired humor in her eyes. Embarrassment flickered through him.

"Sorry," he said, placing the phone on the table. "I am listening."

He meant it, but the device still buzzed with notifications. His gaze drifted toward it.

His sister covered the screen with a napkin. "Try leaving it face down," she suggested. "Just until dessert."

He laughed but agreed.

For the rest of the meal, he did not see the screen light up. He heard full sentences, noticed the way her hands moved when she spoke and how she paused to find the right words.

He left the restaurant feeling oddly content.

The next morning, he decided to test the idea. During his first meeting of the day, he placed his phone face down. He felt its vibration once or twice, but without the visual flash, his attention stayed in the room.

He noticed a colleague's nervousness before a presentation and offered quiet encouragement. His boss's appreciation landed more clearly. The meeting ended faster than usual because fewer people were half distracted.

Rafi did not swear off his phone entirely. He still enjoyed messages, media and the easy companionship of digital life. But he began choosing times to turn it face down and leave it that way.

On train rides, he sometimes watched people instead of timelines. During walks, he let his thoughts wander without interruption.

The change was subtle. No one commented on it. Yet he felt the texture of his days shift.

He caught more small moments. The barista's new haircut. The neighbor's blooming balcony plant. The quiet relief in his sister's voice when he remembered details she had shared weeks earlier.

One night, as he placed his phone face down before bed, he realised the real transformation was not in the object but in his attention. He was learning to let silence fill gaps that had once felt unbearable.

It was not dramatic. It was simply different.

Sometimes the most significant change is choosing where you look when time slows down.

The Note on the Fridge

On the first day of the new year, Ari wrote a single sentence on a sticky note and placed it on her fridge.

Be gentle with yourself, especially when you forget to be.

She had written similar resolutions before. Usually they faded from her mind by February. This time, she did not treat it as a resolution. She treated it as a reminder.

The note was not fancy. Crooked handwriting on pale yellow paper. It curled slightly at the corners when steam from cooking rose.

When she rushed through mornings, she barely saw

it. But on days when she moved more slowly, it caught her eye.

The first time it truly mattered was after a mistake at work. She had missed an important email and delayed a project. Her chest tightened. The familiar inner voice rose, ready with criticism.

You always do this. You are careless. You never learn.

At home that evening, she opened the fridge automatically. The note stared back at her.

Be gentle with yourself, especially when you forget to be.

She read it aloud. The harsh voice inside her quieted, surprised.

She did not excuse the mistake. She sent the necessary apologies, fixed what she could and adjusted her system so the same error would be less likely. But she skipped the part where she called herself names.

Weeks later, when she skipped a planned exercise session, the note met her again. When she burned dinner. When she snapped at a friend and needed to apologise. Each time, it suggested a different path than the familiar spiral of self blame.

Slowly, the sentence became part of her internal language. When she felt stress rise, she sometimes heard herself think, Be gentle, and knew where the phrase had grown from.

She started writing similar notes and placing them in other corners of her life. A card by her bed that said, You are allowed to rest. A bookmark that read, Start again on the next page. A small scrap of paper in her wallet that whispered, You have survived every hard day so far.

She did not show these notes to others on purpose. They were not declarations. They were private signposts.

One afternoon, a friend visited and opened the fridge. She leaned closer to the note and smiled softly.

"I needed to see this," the friend said. "Can I take a picture?"

Ari hesitated, then nodded. As her friend snapped the photo, Ari realised the reminder was big enough to share.

By the end of the year, the original sticky note had faded. The ink was lighter, the paper slightly torn. Ari replaced it with a fresh one, writing the same sentence in clearer ink.

The transformation in her life was not sudden. It arrived word by small word, each time she chose gentleness over old habits.

Sometimes change looks like the same simple note, read again and again, until its truth finally feels real.

The Walk She Took in the Rain

Naomi disliked rain. She planned her days around avoiding it, mapping out covered walkways and timing her errands between showers. One gray afternoon, while leaving the library, the clouds broke open without warning. She stood beneath the awning, frustrated and cold.

The storm was not violent. Just steady, quiet rain falling in diagonal sheets.

She waited five minutes, then ten. Her bus would not arrive for another twenty. She could remain irritated or she could walk.

Naomi stepped into the rain.

The first sensation surprised her. The air felt gentle. The sound around her softened the city's usual noise. Water rolled down her jacket in clear beads. Her hair grew damp in seconds, but she felt no rush to escape.

As she walked slowly down the familiar street, she saw details she usually missed. Leaves trembling under droplets. Reflections shimmering on the pavement. A pigeon shaking out its feathers like a tiny guardian of the sidewalk.

Her feet found a natural rhythm. Something inside her unclenched.

At a crosswalk, she noticed a man holding his coat

above his head, muttering at the sky. She almost laughed. She had been that person countless times.

She continued walking until her bus stop came into view. Instead of waiting, she kept going. The rain felt like a thin curtain lifting something from her thoughts.

By the time she reached home, her shoes were soaked, but her mind was quiet in a way she had not felt for weeks.

Later that evening, as she dried her jacket, Naomi thought about how often she avoided anything uncomfortable. She rarely took chances or tried new routes. She chose predictability out of habit, not preference.

The rain had offered her an accidental moment of freedom. A small act of surrender that changed her relationship with discomfort.

She began allowing more small experiments into her life. Trying unfamiliar cafés. Taking a different street to work. Saying yes to an invitation she would normally decline.

Not every experience was wonderful, but each one expanded her world bit by bit.

Months later, during another gentle storm, she stepped outside deliberately, face turned upward.

Transformation, she realised, sometimes begins by walking straight into the thing you once avoided.

The Morning She Woke Up Rested

For years, Tessa believed productivity measured her worth. Her planner overflowed with tasks, color coded and reorganised weekly. She woke before sunrise, slept long after midnight and judged herself harshly on days when she accomplished little.

Her friends told her she was burning out. She nodded politely, then returned to her list.

One night she worked until her eyes blurred. She set her alarm for five in the morning, then collapsed into bed. The alarm went off hours later, loud and sharp.

She reached for her phone, intending to silence it and rise. Instead, she pressed one button.

Snooze.

The decision felt accidental. But when the alarm sounded again, she pressed snooze a second time. Then a third.

Tessa did not wake properly until eight thirty. Sunlight filtered through the curtains. Birdsong drifted through the window. For the first time in months, her body felt rested.

Panic arrived instantly.

She rushed into the kitchen, grabbed her planner and began flipping through pages, heart racing at the thought of lost time. Then something unusual happened.

She paused.

Her body felt good. Her mind felt clear. She could move without the heaviness that usually clung to her mornings.

She set the planner down.

"What if this is not failure," she whispered. "What if this is repair."

The thought startled her. She made breakfast slowly. She noticed the smell of toasted bread, the warmth of the mug in her hands, the quiet softness of the morning she had been sleeping through for years.

Her workday still began, but she approached it differently. She completed tasks steadily instead of frantically. She declined a meeting she did not need to attend. She took a short walk at lunch.

That night, she turned her alarm off entirely.

Over the next weeks, she allowed herself more rest. Not laziness, but true restoration. She slept longer. She paused more often. She learned the rhythm of her own energy.

The world did not fall apart. Nothing collapsed. In fact, she found herself accomplishing more with far less panic.

One morning she woke rested again and smiled at the sunlight on her blanket. Rest had become not a rare accident but a welcomed companion.

Her planner changed too. Pages that had once held fifty tasks now held ten. She no longer glorified exhaustion.

Transformation, she learned, can begin with something as small as pressing snooze and letting the morning catch up to you gently.

The Dinner for One

When Mark's partner moved abroad for work, Mark discovered he had forgotten how to cook for one person. Meals had always been shared. Conversations filled the kitchen. Silence never sat in the chair across from him.

For weeks, he relied on takeout and cereal. The idea of planning and preparing a proper meal felt pointless.

One Friday evening, after a long workday, he opened the fridge and sighed at its emptiness. Something inside him nudged.

Cook something simple.

He boiled pasta, chopped tomatoes, grated cheese and seasoned everything with herbs he found at the back of a drawer. The kitchen smelled warm and familiar. He set the table with a single plate and a glass of water.

Sitting down felt strange at first. Too quiet. Too still.

But somewhere between the first and second bite, he relaxed. The food tasted better than expected. The silence no longer felt accusatory. It felt peaceful.

He realised he had been treating meals alone as evidence of lack. As if solitude erased the value of nourishment.

The next night, he cooked again. A stir fry. Then a soup. Then a dish he had always relied on his partner to prepare. Each time, he set a place for himself with care. Not extravagantly, but intentionally.

He began enjoying the ritual. Slicing vegetables became meditative. Stirring broth felt grounding. He even bought a small vase and placed a single flower at the center of the table.

One evening, he video called his partner while cooking. She smiled at the sight of the set table.

"You are taking care of yourself," she said. "I am proud of you."

Mark felt warmth spread in his chest.

Cooking for one no longer symbolised loneliness. It became a quiet affirmation that he mattered as much alone as he did in company.

Transformation often starts with a simple act of hospitality turned inward.

The Lesson She Took Twice

Cora enrolled in a pottery class after years of saying she would try it someday. On the first day, the instructor demonstrated how to center clay on the wheel. Cora mimicked her movements, but her clay wobbled wildly.

She tried again. Still lopsided.

Her classmates formed smooth bowls while hers collapsed into uneven heaps.

At the end of the session, she looked at her misshapen piece and felt foolish. Maybe she was not meant for this. She almost decided not to return.

That night, she washed clay from her hands and thought about how often she quit after a single failed attempt. She had done the same with dance, with knitting, with learning Spanish.

She heard the instructor's words echo from earlier: Clay learns you at the same time you learn it.

The next week, Cora returned.

She sat at her wheel and breathed slowly before touching the clay. She paid attention to the sensations under her palms. The clay yielded, then resisted, then softened again.

Her first attempt was still uneven. Her second was slightly better. Her third held shape for a few seconds before slumping.

She laughed instead of groaning.

By the fourth week, she shaped a small bowl that held its form. It was not perfect, but it was undeniably a bowl.

She brought it home and placed it on her dresser. Every time she looked at it, she felt a quiet pride that had nothing to do with skill.

It came from choosing to return.

Months later, she enrolled in the next level class. She still struggled with centering the clay, but she no longer judged herself for it. She found joy in the process rather than the result.

One of her classmates complimented her persistence. "I nearly quit after my first attempt," she said.

Cora smiled. "So did I."

Transformation, she realised, sometimes comes from taking the same lesson twice and letting the second attempt be gentler than the first.

The Card She Never Sent

Rina bought the greeting card on a whim. It featured a watercolor of two foxes curled together in snow. She intended to send it to a friend she had drifted from, someone she still cared about but no longer knew how to approach.

For weeks, the card sat on her desk. She picked it up often, turning it over in her hands, trying to decide what to write.

Every message she drafted felt either too heavy or too light.

Hope you are well.

I miss you.

I am sorry things faded.

Would you like to talk?

She wrote and erased, wrote and erased, until the surface of her notebook page became a gray blur.

One evening she held the blank card and realised she was trying to control every possible outcome. She wanted the message to open a door but feared it might reopen old hurt.

She set the card down and breathed.

Maybe the card did not need to be sent. Maybe its purpose was to help her acknowledge that the friendship mattered, even if the chapter had closed quietly.

She wrote a message inside anyway. Not for her friend, but for herself.

Thank you for the years we shared. I carry the good parts with me.

She signed her name, then placed the card in a drawer.

The act brought unexpected relief. She felt the weight of indecision lift. She no longer needed to choose between silence and risk. She had honored the relationship privately, in a way that felt true.

Over the next days, she noticed a shift. She stopped replaying old conversations. She released the guilt she had been holding. She felt gratitude instead of regret.

Weeks later, she ran into her old friend at a bookstore. They greeted each other warmly. The conversation was easy, gentle, free of the tension she had feared.

As they parted, her friend said, "It was really good to see you."

"It was good to see you too," Rina replied.

She went home and opened the drawer. The card was still there, quiet and complete.

Some transformations happen not when a message is sent, but when it is finally understood.

The Shoes Beside the Door

Daniel kept two pairs of shoes by his front door. One comfortable pair for errands, and one pair of running shoes he had not worn in over a year. Every time he left the house, he stepped over them.

Each time, he felt a small sting of guilt.

He used to run almost daily, not competitively, but for the clarity it gave him. After a minor injury, he stopped. The injury healed long ago, but the habit did not return. The shoes became symbols of a past self he felt uncertain he could reclaim.

One morning, while rushing out, he tripped slightly on the running shoes. The stumble was small, but the annoyance lingered.

Daniel stared at the shoes. "You are not helping," he muttered.

That evening, he sat beside them and untied the laces on both pairs. The running shoes felt stiff from disuse. He picked them up and considered throwing them out, but something held him back.

He placed them outside on the balcony to air. The next morning, he cleaned them gently with warm water and set them by the door again.

He did not run. He simply prepared.

Two days later, he walked a short route in them. Not a run. Not a goal. Just a test. The shoes felt unfamiliar, but not unfriendly.

The following week, he jogged for two minutes, then walked the rest of the way home. He felt winded but proud. He did not promise himself anything grand. He simply tried again the next day, and the next.

Gradually, he found a new rhythm. Faster than walking, slower than his old pace. It felt more like moving forward than trying to reclaim something lost.

One morning, as he approached the door, he realised the guilt was gone. He no longer stepped over the shoes. He stepped into them.

He did not run every day. He did not set targets or compete with his past self. He simply ran when it felt right. The shoes were no longer symbols of failure. They were companions in renewal.

Transformation, he learned, sometimes begins with picking up something you thought you had abandoned and letting it belong to you in a new way.

The Garden Gate

Behind Lina's apartment building stood a small community garden. Residents could volunteer to tend a plot, but Lina always felt too inexperienced. She admired the flowers from a distance, assuming the gardeners belonged to a group she was not part of.

One afternoon, while carrying groceries home, she noticed the garden gate swinging open. A gentle breeze moved through the rows of plants, stirring the leaves.

She hesitated, then stepped inside.

The air smelled of soil and rosemary. Bees drifted lazily between blossoms. A woman in a sun hat kneeled by a raised bed, pulling weeds with slow, patient movements.

"You are welcome to wander," the woman said without looking up.

Lina smiled nervously. "I am not a gardener."

"Everyone begins as a non gardener," the woman replied. "Would you like to help with these weeds?"

Lina set her grocery bag aside and knelt beside her. They worked quietly, hands brushing soil. The woman introduced herself as Mara, one of the garden's founders. She explained how each plot was shared, how volunteers came and went, how plants often grew in unexpected combinations.

"Gardens forgive inconsistency," Mara said. "They only ask for small, regular care."

Lina listened, surprised by how calming the simple task felt.

Over the next weeks, she returned often. Sometimes to weed. Sometimes to water. Sometimes just to sit among the plants and breathe more deeply than she could in her apartment.

The garden became a place where she could think without pressure. She noticed subtle changes. A sprout appearing where none had been. A flower opening overnight. A tomato ripening slowly.

She applied the same gentle patience to her own life. She let friendships evolve instead of forcing them. She took breaks before reaching exhaustion. She allowed space for slow progress in her work.

One morning, Mara handed her a small packet of seeds. "Your own patch is ready," she said. "Nothing complicated. Herbs to begin with."

Lina felt a wave of quiet joy.

She planted them carefully, unsure if they would flourish. Weeks later, the first green shoots appeared. She knelt beside them, smiling at the fragile beginnings.

The transformation was not just the garden's growth. It was the shift in how she saw herself. Someone capable of tending. Someone allowed to start small. Someone who did not need permission to belong.

Sometimes a single open gate is enough to change the shape of a life.

The Old Sweater

The navy sweater had belonged to Rowan's grandfather. It was soft with age, elbows slightly worn, cuffs loose from years of use. She kept it folded at the foot of her bed but rarely wore it, afraid it might fall apart.

Whenever she felt lonely or overwhelmed, she would

run her hand over its fabric. It comforted her in a way nothing else quite did.

One chilly evening, after a difficult phone call, she wrapped the sweater around herself. It smelled faintly of cedar and something she associated with childhood winters.

As she sat in the quiet, she realised she had been treating the sweater like a relic rather than a source of warmth. Her grandfather had never believed in keeping things unused. He repaired, patched, rebuilt. He gave objects long lives by letting them live, not by storing them away.

Rowan stood and looked at herself in the mirror. The sweater hung comfortably. She felt wrapped not just in fabric, but in memory and care.

She wore it the next day while reading on the balcony. She wore it while writing postcards, while carrying groceries, while drinking tea with a friend who said, "You look peaceful today."

The sweater's threads loosened slightly with each wear, but Rowan found comfort in that. Life was meant to be lived in, not preserved in glass.

One morning, she noticed a small tear near the wrist. Instead of panicking, she found her grandfather's old sewing kit and stitched it carefully. Her stitches were uneven, but she felt him close in the act.

Each time she mended a small flaw, she imagined she was stitching a conversation across time.

Months passed. The sweater grew more worn, but so did her fear of losing what mattered. She realised that using something precious did not diminish it. It deepened its meaning.

When a friend asked why she wore it so often, Rowan smiled. "Because it reminds me that care is not fragile. It stretches."

Quiet transformation often happens when we stop protecting our memories like fragile antiques and start letting them support our everyday lives.

The Window She Cleaned Last

Meera planned to spend Saturday cleaning her apartment. She scrubbed the counters, swept the floors and sorted laundry. Only one task remained: the small window above her kitchen sink.

She had ignored it for months. The glass was cloudy with dust and streaked from old rain. She rarely looked through it, convinced the view was uninteresting. It faced a narrow alley and the brick wall of the neighboring building.

Near sunset, she filled a bowl with soapy water and pulled the curtain aside. As she began wiping the glass, the grime cleared slowly, revealing a sharper image of the alley below.

She paused. A balcony she had never noticed before jutted out from the opposite building. On it sat a row of potted plants, green and thriving. Small lanterns hung from the railing. Wind chimes swayed gently.

Someone cared for that space with attention.

As Meera continued cleaning, she saw more. A painted ceramic bird perched on one pot. A tiny windmill spinning lazily. A bright blue watering can shaped like a fish.

She found herself smiling.

The neighbor stepped onto the balcony a moment later. An older woman with silver hair tied in a loose braid. She watered the plants with slow, practiced motions.

Without thinking, Meera tapped the window lightly. The woman looked up, startled, then waved warmly before returning to her plants.

Meera felt her chest warm with unexpected connection.

The alley, once dismissed as dreary, now held a pocket of life. She could not believe she had ignored it simply because the window looked dirty.

Over the next days, she opened the curtain more often. Sometimes she caught glimpses of the woman reading on the balcony or humming to her plants. Sometimes the balcony was empty, but the sight of the greenery still soothed her.

Inspired, Meera placed a small plant of her own on her windowsill. Then another. Soon the once neglected window became her favorite spot in the kitchen.

One afternoon, she returned home to find a note stuck to the outside of the glass.

Your plants look lovely. Thank you for brightening the view.

Meera wrote a reply on a sticky note and pressed it to the same spot. They exchanged small messages for weeks. Nothing elaborate. Just brief greetings and compliments.

The transformation had not come from cleaning alone. It came from choosing to look through a place she once avoided, discovering beauty in the last window she had bothered to wipe.

Sometimes change begins with clearing a view you never thought to notice.

The Call She Answered

Lila's phone rang during dinner. An unknown number. Her instinct was to let it go to voicemail. She preferred predictable conversations with familiar people. Unknown numbers usually meant noise, not meaning.

The phone rang again.

Something nudged her. She answered.

A soft voice greeted her. "Is this Lila Parker?"

"Yes," she said cautiously.

"This is Marianne from the community center. You listed yourself as an emergency contact for a neighbor, Mr. Alden. He is fine, but he slipped during an exercise class and asked us to call someone to help him home."

Lila blinked. She had listed herself on a whim years earlier, shortly after moving into the building. Mr. Alden had once helped her carry a heavy package, and she had signed her name on a volunteer sheet without expecting to be needed.

"I can come," she said.

At the center, she found him sitting with his leg elevated, smiling sheepishly.

"I did not want to worry my daughter," he said. "She lives too far for a quick visit."

Lila helped him into a taxi and supported him up the stairs to his apartment. He insisted she stay for tea, so she did.

He told her stories about his late wife, about the neighborhood before it became filled with cafes, about the years he worked at the post office. His voice carried the gentle rhythm of someone grateful for company.

Lila found herself relaxing. She realised she had kept her world small by avoiding interactions that might surprise her.

When she left, he said, "Thank you for answering. Most people screen their calls."

"So do I," she admitted. "Usually."

Over the next week, she checked on him every few days, bringing groceries or sharing short conversations. She learned he liked crossword puzzles, disliked cauliflower and played the harmonica surprisingly well.

One evening, as they drank tea, he said, "You know, you helped more than you think. Not just with the fall. With the days after."

Lila felt a quiet shift inside. She had never thought of herself as someone who made a difference in another person's routine. Her life often felt solitary and unremarkable.

Walking back to her apartment, she realised she felt lighter. The call she almost ignored had become a hinge in her week, opening a door to connection she had not known she needed.

From then on, she answered unknown numbers more often. Not every call led to something meaningful. But she felt less afraid of surprise.

Transformation, she discovered, sometimes begins with saying hello to someone you did not expect.

Afterword: The Quiet Work of Small Stories

Every book has a journey of its own, even one made of very small pieces. When I began writing the stories in this collection, I thought I was simply gathering little moments, brief sparks that could stand on their own. What became clear along the way was that micro stories do not stand alone at all. They reach out toward one another. They speak across pages. They echo in subtle ways. They form a larger story that takes shape only once the reader steps inside and begins to wander.

Writing micro fiction is a study in attention. It demands listening not just to language but to silence, to pauses, to what a sentence implies without saying. Most of the time, the process feels like tuning a signal. A story begins with an image or a feeling, something fragile enough to disappear if handled roughly. The task is to hold it gently, to translate it into words without weighing it down. The shorter the piece, the more carefully each word must be chosen. A story of three hundred words carries no space for hesitation. Every detail earns its place or steps aside.

There is a particular kind of discipline in shaping something so brief. A long story can wander and return. A short one must walk with intention from its first line. Yet this constraint is freeing. When a story knows exactly how much room it has, it discovers what truly matters. The process becomes one of distillation. You cut away what is almost right in search of what is exactly right. You learn to trust the reader to complete the picture. You learn to trust suggestion over explanation. Micro fiction is an act of collaboration between writer and reader. Half of the meaning lives in the space where those two imaginations meet.

This book followed me through seasons, and I always knew it would find its home in winter. The themes were chosen early, but they deepened during the writing. Hope became more than a concept. It became a compass. Winter magic revealed itself in the quietest hours of cold mornings. Serendipity announced itself through coincidences that arrived while drafting. Quiet transformation unfolded slowly, not only on the page but in thought. In this sense, the book grew in the same way the stories within it grow. Through small steps, subtle shifts, and unexpected alignments.

Hope is an emotion that refuses to be simplified. It can feel bright, but it can also feel heavy. It carries both possibility and ache. The stories in the first section taught me to pay closer attention to the kinds of hope that do not shout. The hope that appears in tired eyes. The hope woven into a simple routine. The hope that flickers even when nothing dramatic has changed. Writing those pieces reminded me that hope is a practice, not a conclusion. It is something we choose, again and again, even when we do not feel brave.

Winter magic offered a different lesson. During the writing of that section, I found myself stopping more often to watch how the world shifts in cold air. The quiet of winter teaches patience. It teaches the value of noticing. A single sound becomes clearer. A single memory becomes sharper. Even the smallest movement seems meaningful. Writing stories about winter is a way of honoring that stillness. It invites the reader to pause too, to let the season speak in its own slow rhythm.

Serendipity arrived unexpectedly. Many of the stories in that section emerged from moments of chance in my own days. A misplaced note. A conversation overheard. A small accident that led to a new idea. Serendipity reminds us that life rarely unfolds in straight lines. It bends and loops. It surprises us. The stories in this section celebrate that gentle unpredictability. They suggest that even the smallest encounter can alter a path. Writing them encouraged me to look at my own life with a softer lens. To see coincidence not as chaos but as invitation.

Quiet transformations, the final theme, carried me through the end of the project. Transformation is a word that often calls to mind grand changes, but I have learned that the most profound shifts happen quietly. They happen in the spaces between thoughts. They happen when we release an old belief or recognise a new truth. They happen when a person decides, without fanfare, to choose kindness or courage or clarity. Writing the closing stories showed me how tender those moments can be. They are not dramatic. They are real. They shape us more than we realise.

If this book has a single thread running through all four sections, it is the idea that small things matter. A short story can hold an entire world in a single image. A passing moment can change the direction of a day. A subtle thought can reshape a life. We often look for meaning in the large and the loud, but meaning often hides in the quiet corners. In the slight shift of tone in a conversation. In the way light falls on a familiar place. In the decision to take one step forward when it feels easier not to move at all.

Readers bring their own stories into any book, but they bring an especially powerful presence into micro fiction. Because the form is open and compressed, it needs the reader to expand it, to breathe into the spaces between sentences. Your experiences, your memories, your joys and your losses complete these stories in ways I cannot. Once a piece is written, it belongs half to me and half to you. Together we make it whole. That is the quiet magic of this form.

As you reach the end of this collection, I hope you carry something with you. Not only the stories but the way they asked you to slow down, to look closely, to listen. I hope something here has brightened a moment or touched a memory. I hope a particular sentence lingers with you, or a character stays in your thoughts, or a small image opens into something larger when you least expect it.

Thank you for spending time with these stories. Thank you for meeting them with attention and care. Thank you for allowing them to become part of your inner landscape, even for a short while. Writing a book is an act of faith. Reading one is too. I am grateful for your company on this journey through hope, winter light, unexpected turns and quiet change.

If these stories leave you with anything, let it be this: small moments matter. They shape us. They guide us. They offer comfort, wonder and renewal. The world is full of them. The world is full of stories waiting to be noticed.

May you continue to find them. And may they continue to find you.